Unlikely Barons

Murray Hall

Leschenault
PRESS
Great Stories from Great Writers

Copyright © Murray Hall, 2022

Published: 2022 by Leschenault Press
Leschenault, Western Australia

ISBN: 9781922670892 - Hardback Edition
        9781922670908 - Paperback
        9781922670915 - eBook

***

Cover Design by Brittany Wilson | Brittwilsonart.com
Cover Photos by Jodie Craig | www.samanthamay.com.au

A catalogue record for this book is available from the National Library of Australia

Dedicated to the memory of my father
David (Ernie) Hall

This book was inspired by true events.
Allegedly…

If you lived in Broome in the 1990's,
are offended by bad language, sex or drugs
shut the cover now and step away from this book.

Pindan (noun):
*Arid, sandy country characteristic of the southwest Kimberley region of Western
Australia. "The savanna is surrounded by an extensive stretch of pindan."*

Origin:
Late 19th century: from Bardi (an Aboriginal language) bindan 'the bush'.

Other Aussie terms are in the glossary at the back if you need some
help with the quaint vocabulary of our nation.

Language Warning: Seriously, just in case you missed it above, this
book contains swear words. A lot of them. If you are okay with that,
read on. If not, then probably best you f*** off.

Also by Murray Hall

Non-Fiction
As Murray Ernest Hall

Walk a War in My Shoes

Wooroloo Prison Farm 2017

The Kat's second wife decided that after his sentencing she had other things to do in life. She cleaned the house out, keeping enough quality furniture for her new apartment and carefully went through the floor safe contents, pocketing half the $35,000 in cash and all the jewellery.

As she left the city, she dropped their 11-year-old Labrador, Ringo and the house keys off at a mate's place.

A week later a solicitor's letter was sent to Kat advising him of the separation, notice of intention to divorce, a claim for half the value of the family home and a request that he transfer ownership of the black 2016 Mercedes-Benz C200 two-door coupe into her name.

***

I hadn't seen Kat for a decade, no dummy spit, people just grow apart, everyone has their own issues to take care of and good mates drift to be good acquaintances. It's the cycle of life.

We had all moved out of Broome at different times for different reasons in the late 90's. We settled back in, or close to, Perth where the tropical heat couldn't get us.

A regular regime of long lunches that turned into even longer piss-ups struggled on for a few years. The Dodger was there for some of them, but he moved around a bit and wasn't always in town. Over time the gap between the reunions stretched out. Eventually they stopped altogether.

So, in April 2017, the last thing I expected was to get a phone call from a withheld number and a bloke I didn't know, claiming to be a mate of Kat's.

"What can I do for you?" I asked.

"Would you mind swinging past Wooroloo Prison when you're next in the area?"

"What for?"

"Kat's in there and he wants to see you."

Before I got the chance to say anything, he added, "Oh and maybe tell him, Ringo's dead."

I had a lot of questions, but the caller had already hung up. Staring at my smart phone for a moment I opened the map app to find Wooroloo was 120 kilometres from my house. Strangely, in all my time as a journalist I'd never visited a prison. I guess there's a first time for everything but I figured you couldn't simply rock up and ask to see an inmate, so a quick Google search later and I'd pre-booked a time slot for the following week.

On Saturday afternoon, after passing through security checks and having a drug dog sniff my nuts, I took a seat at an outside table on the visitors' lawn. After a few minutes I watched an old guy shuffling towards me, he was rubbing his hands over his bald head and his British racing green overalls hung loose on his withered frame. I felt sorry for the old bastard until he sat down opposite me.

"G'day Aaron."

I managed not to say, "Fuck me, Kat, what the hell happened to you." Instead, I stumbled over, "Mate, good to see ya, you're looking good."

"And you're full of shit, but it's good to see you too."

"So what are you in here for?" I asked.

"Very funny. You didn't know?"

"No mate, don't have a clue."

That's not quite true, I'd looked him up through Perth Magistrate Court records.

"The Jacks finally got me enough times for DUI. I'd have got away with it if I'd not hit the two parked cars."

I laughed. "How long you in for?"

"Six months down, three to go if I don't get caught going over the back fence first. I've got a couple of neighbours in my street and an insurance company on my case over the damage bill. But they can wait."

My attention was diverted by a drug-fucked female with one front tooth giving her inmate boyfriend a hand job at the next table.

I hadn't seen that activity on the list of what not to do while visiting a prisoner but figured it probably wasn't allowed.

My suspicions were confirmed when a prison guard walked up from behind and gave the bloke a tap on the head.

Being that violence is forbidden by both sides, it was only a light tap, it didn't fracture his skull or put him in a coma.

"Put it away now or she goes out the front gate and you go to Casuarina."

The inmate said nothing and I guessed I knew why. Wooroloo Prison Farm even on its worse day was probably a laid-back place compared to Casuarina high security.

Unfortunately for him, his eloquent girlfriend arced up and proceeded to teach the kids in the visiting compound words they wouldn't learn at Sunday school.

Two more guards arrived and the good lady was led away kicking and screaming.

Kat rolled his eyes and waited for the commotion to die down and circus to leave town.

He leant towards me and beckoned me to do the same.

"How long we known each other for mate?"

I had the flash of a memory. Me standing in the Pearl Function room of the Broome Shire Offices, a reporter's notepad in hand and my photographer colleague, Rick, alongside. We were there to cover the monthly Business After-Hours Sundowner, a thankless task always assigned to the newest journalist at the Broome Observer. Fifteen minutes into my first experience of the Broome social scene and I was bored shitless already.

I nudged Rick and tilted my head towards the bar at the end of the room. He lifted his Nikon 35mm camera and inclined his own head towards the two 30-something brunettes making inroads into a badly concealed bottle of Bourbon. I noticed their short hemlines and low-cut blouses and considered doing one more interview but figured I needed another Swan Premium to set me up.

Arriving at the bar, I stood next to two blokes about the same age as me. They looked a bit upmarket to most of the other punters in the room. Clean shaven and with a whiff of L'Occitane eau de toilette mixed with some face moisturiser I couldn't place. For a second I wondered if one of them was the new Mayor.

Both were taller and broader than I was but all three of us were wearing what appeared to be the Broome after hour's uniform of black shoes, cotton pants, ironed white shirt, no tie. We weren't in the Perth Yacht Club, we were north of the 26th parallel and the average evening temperature was 30°C.

The closest man to me said something but I didn't quite catch it. He turned to the girl behind the bar, "Can you take the edge off the music please. I can't hear myself think down this end of the room."

As the strains of UB40's latest number one were turned down the man tried again.

"You the new journo?"

I lifted my reporter's notepad and said, "Yep, for my sins. I'm Aaron, do you fancy having a chat?"

His mate leant around and said, "Fuck off mate. All we want's a beer."

The pair of them laughed and introduced themselves as Kat and Dodger. Six hours later, sitting at the outside smoko table of their business yard, we had finished off a carton of Swan Premium and started on the best of friendships.

I came back to the table at Wooroloo a little shocked at my answer for Kat. "Bloody hell, we met in '93. That's 24 years, mate… Why?"

"And do you still trust me?"

"Of course."

"Good. I need you to do me a favour."

The Journalist

It wasn't until the aircraft was on final approach to the Kimberley town of Broome that I realised I had forgotten to tell Kat his dog was dead. I took my mind off it by looking out the window. The aircraft banked over the Indian Ocean and afforded a view of the tropical town site that was gateway to the Kimberley jewels like Cape Leveque, the Bungle Bungle's, Horizontal Falls, Ord River, El Questro, Lake Argyle and a hundred other "bucket list" venues. It was strange being back after all these years and I wondered how much the place would have changed.

In 1993 Broome was seen by many, me included, as the Wild West. Not only for its remoteness to the rest of Australia and its savage heat, but more for its rough as guts laid-back, she'll be right, semi-policed, transient, free loader, dole bludging, piss head, pot-smoking population. All of them living between the turquoise blue water of Roebuck Bay, Gantheaume Point and Cable Beach, arguably the best tropical beach in the world.

Yet for all its beauty some of its history was ugly. I had first arrived 110 years after Sir Fredrick Broome had declared the town and named it after himself, thereby ignoring the potential 30,000 years of local indigenous habitation. Truth be told when I arrived as a young journalist not much had changed on that score.

The town had thrived based on the pearling industry, growing throughout the 1880's but it had a dark existence with the use of slave labour, mostly Asians. Many racially motivated conflicts arose over the years which climaxed with the death of eight people and many more injured when the Japanese and Malay inhabitants rioted in 1920.

Racial segregation still existed in the region into the early 70's which was a hangover from the unique situation of the town never having been party to the White Australia Policy.

As I drove down Frederick Street now, I was greeted by a thriving, clean, well-laid out, modern town. It would still rely on the tourist dollar, but I couldn't blame them for that. I slowed to allow for recreational vehicles and a 4x4 towing one of the biggest caravans I'd ever seen out of a carpark in front of the local camping supply shop. These were the grey nomads, a constant feature of the town since I'd lived here. It was good to see somethings hadn't changed. I had to hope that the destination I was heading to also remained the same as Kat had described.

Continuing south I eventually turned left into Clementson Street. The road was lined with various industrial units housing everything from a meat packing company to a smash repair yard. At the end of the street before it turned back north into the town centre was a two-acre derelict yard surrounded by well-maintained security fencing. Amidst the cracked concrete, fractured with free-growing spinifex, sat a 40m square, heavily rusted, corrugated iron shed topped with a sun-faded green Colorbond roof blotched with the signature red of pindan dust; a trademark of the buildings in the town. I pulled up in front of an impressively padlocked gate and took a breath to prepare myself for stepping out of my air-conditioned car and into the heat of a Broome May.

The padlock was a six-tumbler combination the likes of which I'd seen only on customs sealed containers at Perth International Airport. I flicked the digits to the combination Kat had told me back in the prison, 231163. The lock clicked open.

Swinging the gates back I retrieved my car and drove it across to the shed. There was no impressive lock on the main roller door because you could have kicked it in due to the amount of rust on it. Taking my backpack from the boot of the car I went inside and left the roller door half up to provide some light and hopefully some airflow. The inside of the shed felt like the worst sweatbox imaginable, but the interior was exactly as Kat had described.

An accommodation donga filled the north-west corner and sat on a chassis made up of 200mm x 100mm, rectangular hollow section, galvanised steel. In the north-east corner was another donga which, back in the day, had been an administration office. It sat on a chassis that had a spare wheel attached to a swing bracket like I'd seen on many a grey nomad's caravan. However, the wheel's tyre had been slashed so it wasn't much use to anyone. Reaching into my backpack I took out a battery operated 5' grinder fitted with a 3mm steel cutting blade.

I could have brought it with me as hold luggage on the plane, but it had been just as easy buying it from the local Bunnings when I arrived. Glancing back over my shoulder towards the roller door, checking that I was still alone, I reached for my other purchases and slipped on a pair of safety glasses and a dust mask. Powering up the grinder I cut through the industrial padlock that held the wheel's swing bracket closed. Grabbing the rim of the tire and leaning my full weight back I struggled to pull the bracket from the position it had held for almost 15 years.

Eventually with a screaming reluctance, metal scrapped across metal and the hollow end of the main steel chassis was revealed. Using my smart phone torch, I easily found the thin piece of metal welding wire Kat had told me to expect to find inside. Pulling it gently I walked backwards for five metres until the clatter of a metal cash box hitting the ground stopped me.

The lid of the cash box flipped open and the reason I'd come all this way fell onto the concrete. I stepped forward and lifted a small black velvet drawstring bag and a dusty leather bound A5 journal.

"It depends what you want as a favour?" I'd asked Kat as we sat at the table in Wooroloo.

"I want you to go to Broome and find my diary."

"Would never have taken you for a Samuel Pepys type."

"Who?"

"Never mind. So, you've got a diary and it's in Broome. You want me to do what with it?"

"You're still connected with that publisher? Still doing ghost writing?"

"Off and on. Sometimes, why?"

"Because I want you to find my diary and write my biography."

"Sure, but it'll cost ya. I don't work for nothing."

"That's okay. Payment's not a problem. But, mate… you can't publish it yet."

"And when can I?"

Kat had looked up and down the length of his own body and shrugged at me. "Doctors reckon maybe six months' time."

"Why not sooner? Why not before?"

"You'll know why when you read it."

Two weeks later, as I walked over to the roller door and opened the diary, it didn't take me long to understand.

Kat's Diary

If you lived in Broome in the early 90's, one way or another, you were probably doing okay. There would be a fair chance that you actually wanted to be there. It offered up an idyllic lifestyle, living the dream on the edge of the desert, magnificent blue sky, pristine beaches you could drive your car along for hours or lay naked on the sand soaking up the outstanding weather.

If you were chasing a quid there was plenty of work on and if you had a bit of grunt and drive in you, there were a million opportunities to improve your circumstances. You just needed to be a bit sharp and sometimes being in the right place at the right time helped.

Dodger and I fitted the mould perfectly.

We'd both stumbled into town on the back of marriage breakups with kids involved, not sulking nor suffering from depression or mental breakdowns but admittedly, a bit wounded. In my case I was trying to clear my head and seek out a different direction in life.

I found a job within a few days, working as a contractor, doing a bit of welding and fabrication work.

Being a contractor was a tax dodge. You got paid well above the mandated rate and you were responsible for your own tax affairs. In other words it was up to you to pay the tax due on your income to the Australian Tax Office. The ATO didn't care until you told them how much you had earnt for the year.

The downside was that there was no holiday pay, no superannuation, no sick pay, but if you had any sort of work ethic and had your head around the tax laws, it was a great rort.

Dodger and I had known each other from Perth, where our paths had crossed on a few jobs. I wouldn't say we'd been mates, but we'd not been uncomfortable in each other's company.

I'd been in Broome three weeks and it brought a smile to my face when I saw him walk into the yard where I was working. I told the business owner that I knew Dodger and that he was good value.

He got a start alongside me the next day.

I had used his given name in Perth, but on that first day working together in Broome he'd said he was there dodging the ATO. From that day forward he'd always be, 'Dodger'.

We had a bit in common. We were both Perth boys, both had exes who were giving us the shits, both were grafters and we both knew we could do better for ourselves. Although we didn't really look alike, some people thought we were brothers. I guess it was an easy mistake to make. We were similar in height at around six foot, fit, strong, solid and, I suppose, not bad looking with that rough edge the Kimberley living bestowed upon us. It was enough to occasionally confuse people. The biggest difference between us was that Dodger had a full head of hair that would have done Elvis proud. Whereas I had opted for a crew cut. Some people in the Broome elite used to take a back step at my somewhat threatening appearance but thankfully my Perth-based, all-boys Grammar school education allowed me to win them over quite quickly.

After working all day, Dodger and I would go out for a few beers together. That progressed to going to the gym once or twice a week, throwing a few weights around and sparring. He'd had a junior career at State boxing championship level and taught me bits and pieces of that sport that I'd had no prior knowledge of. He never gave me a flogging, but I never doubted he would have been capable of doing so.

You come across a lot of people in your life that you wouldn't piss on if they were on fire, but the Dodger appealed to me, I liked the man.

Six months after we began working together and recognising a massive shortage of skill in the building trade around Broome, we decided to have a crack at it ourselves instead of working for somebody else. We rented a factory, started banging on doors and from scratch built a respectable business that would support our lifestyle.

Over the next 12 months the building trade exploded and we picked up a variety of work all over the place, most of it coming in via house building contractors. As we progressed and our business confidence grew, we expanded into more heavy-duty projects and the business also became a bit of a one-stop-shop for do-it-yourself guys wanting steel products.

Cash flow was a problem in the early stages as neither of us arrived in Broome with a big quid in our pockets, so rapid growth meant pouring as much back into the business as possible to lease forklifts, buy welding equipment, consumables and employ others.

The common business model used around town was the 'she'll be right' attitude and no one was in a hurry to do anything. There was a common term used in Broome called, "Broome Time" and it referred to the laid-back, "I'll do it when I get around to it" temperament. It was a piss-poor attitude and we made a conscious decision to lift our game, doing whatever it took.

Being punctual, working back late, bending over backwards to get a job out on time and priding ourselves on quality workmanship. Our work ethic worked very well for us, as a large percentage of our business came from word-of-mouth referrals and repeat customers.

We were never going to be a threat to a building conglomerate empire, but we were plodding along very nicely. Rolling the factory lease over a year later and negotiating a three-by-three-year deal on the place gave us a bit of security. Before that lease was up, we'd purchased the property.

The opportunity to grow was only limited by the amount of work we could take on and, on a few occasions, we had to decline jobs simply because we were too busy.

We'd established a rapport with councillors, real estate agents and larger builders, rubbing shoulders with the great and good of Broome and mixing in circles that helped us earn a dollar.

As our business grew and our private lives stabilised, Dodger sold the van he had been living in and moved into a place in town with his second missus. For my part I'd leased out a nice three-bedroom joint quite close to him.

In those days Broome had three very clearly separated levels of habitants. The top echelon belonged to the well to do, genuine businesspeople and city administrators, Rotary members, some coppers and the part-time judiciary. Basically, the money and brains end of town, the decision makers.

Of course, there were a few fringe dwellers around that group, but you get the drift.

Second tier and the majority of the fluctuating population was the general work force, the transients and grey nomads. A significant amount of people, (mostly blokes), were there hiding from the law, the Australian Tax Office, their ex-wives, child-support payments or a combination of all of them.

The third tier was the indigenous community, both in town and camps in the outlying areas.

By 1992, Dodger and I sat at the high end of tier two. A respectable spot on the food chain. Anyone looking at us as we came into that summer would have seen a couple of blokes, accepted in the community, operating a well-run business.

What they wouldn't have seen was the rest of our business dealings. For as well as being builders we were the hidden faces of the Broome drug trade and would make more money selling gear in the following 18-months than our legitimate business would have made in 18 years.

Pablo

It wasn't a conscious decision to become drug dealers.

We didn't sit around a table one day thinking that it would be a good idea. It just happened. Bizarrely, it turned out to be no more difficult or complicated than walking up the street and buying the morning paper.

I'd met Pablo five years earlier when I worked with him in Perth. That wasn't his real name obviously, but his family were originally from South America and Pablo Escobar had been all over the news in the late 1980's and I thought it was funny.

Pablo would tell me on a few occasions to wheel it in, so I usually only called him it if we were having a discussion where I needed him to pay attention.

Although only casual acquaintances outside of work, I knew him well enough and, on many occasions, had seen him selling drugs around town as well as to work associates. Being that I had no interest in any drugs whatsoever and never had done, none of this concerned me. I knew nothing about the trade nor was I remotely interested. A couple of times I'd asked about the little plastic zip-top bags with the line of white powder in it. He'd told me what it did, how it was used and how much people paid for it. I was amused at the thought of people paying that much money for the shit but that was as far as my curiosity extended.

On one stinking hot, tropical downpour-laden night in November, '92, with the constant chirping of cicadas providing their usual cacophony to the evening orchestra of car horns and rowdy drinkers being turfed out of the town pubs, I took a call on my new Nokia 6110 mobile phone as I walked up Frederick Street. I was a bit shocked as usually I had to stand on one leg with my arm raised at an angle to get any mobile service at all. To be honest I'd only bought the phone to impress one of the birds in the shire planning office.

Straining to hear the voice on the other end, I finally made out Pablo's dulcet tones and wondered what the fuck he was calling me for.

"I'm coming up to Broome with my missus for a holiday. Fancy catching up for a beer?"

I hadn't even realised he had my number but happily agreed to his invitation.

We met in a pub for dinner and over an average 'Parmi and chips' I asked him jokingly how the drug business was going. He laughed but unsubtly looked over both shoulders before asking me quietly if I was on the gear these days.

"No mate. You know me, I never touched the stuff."

He waved his hand towards the half dozen blokes propping up the bar and said, "I wish I lived here. Most of those blokes would be dead cert customers. I could make a dollar here."

I twisted around taking in a view of the bar. "These blokes? How'd you know that?"

"You kidding? Look at the heads on them. Every one of those blokes is either on it, been on it or looking for it. Honestly, I could turn an ounce or two over here in about an hour every Friday."

In the middle of another mouthful of chips I managed to mumble, "What's an ounce?"

"Between two and three large at retail price is what an ounce is mate and eighty percent of that's pure profit."

Slowly cutting another piece of my Parmi, I let my mental arithmetic do the maths. A large building job for me and Dodger over the course of a 40-hour week brought us in maybe $1,500 profit, or in Pablo's parlance, one and a half large. I sat back and washed down my chicken with the last of my can of Victorian Bitter. VB wasn't my go-to beer, but Pablo liked it. By the time I sat the empty can back on the table I decided to ask him a question.

"How does it work?"

We went for a walk back to Pablo's holiday let. I was concerned his wife, Maria would ask questions, but he assured me she'd had a migraine and had taken a painkiller strong enough to knock her out for the night.

"Besides," he said, "She's into it as deep as I am, don't worry about her mate."

As we sat in the kitchen dining area at a Formica-covered table, I received a basic schooling in and a glossary of terms for, the Western Australian drug trade. Specifically, the supply and distribution of amphetamines referred to by Pablo as *Go, Goey, Clout, Whippa, Hit, Up, Amp, Speed* and *White*.

Later that night he pulled a footy sock out from under the mattress and emptied the contents onto the table. My eye was caught by a zip-top bag about three inches long, full of powder, not dissimilar in look to plain flour, very fine, almost bright white. It had a very sweet smell to it and I was about to dip my finger in, like I'd seen on cop shows when Pablo grabbed it up.

"What the fuck are you doing?"

"I was gunna taste it like they do on the TV."

"Are you nuts, Kat? You've never used anything ever, have you? You don't even smoke mate, not even Marlboro's. You stick a finger full of that in, you'll be bouncing around for a week."

"Sorry. I just wanted to know what it tastes like."

"It tastes like shit, sour. But unless you're used to taking gear there's better ways to test the quality and anyway if I'm supplying you, I'll be your quality control."

I looked back down at the small bag on the table. "How much is that worth then?"

"That's an ounce of Speed and you'll buy it off me for a grand."

"Bullshit I will. How the hell do I make that sort of money back from an amount that small?"

"You break the ounce up into twenty-eight one-gram bags." He held up a smaller zip-top bag a bit bigger than a postage stamp, "and you sell each one of those for a hunge."

"A what?"

"A hundred bucks, mate. Fuck you are a cleanskin aren't ya."

"What the fuck's wine gotta do with it," I said, my back getting up.

Pablo relaxed back and laughed. "Nah mate. A cleanskin's a drug virgin. No record, no knowledge of the game. Like you. And," he said waving me to calm down, "It's no bad thing. The cops won't have a fuckin' clue where to look."

I shrugged. "Go on."

"Right, well every one of those clowns at the bar would be onto the small amounts you break the ounce into. You sell all of them and you just turned your grand into twenty-eight hundred."

I sat back and let the ever-present sound of ocean waves crashing on the beach calm my thoughts. "People pay one-hundred dollars for that?"

"Absolutely. It's the going rate. Well, a hundred in Perth, put the price up here, one-twenty."

"How do you measure out the quantity?"

He reached back into the footy sock and pulled out a small set of jeweller's scales, smaller than my hand. Step by step he showed me how to put the empty bag on the scales, zero the scales and using a table knife, transfer one gram from the ounce bag into the small bag. Easy as that.

"Okay, it's getting late," I said, stretching my back that had been playing up a bit lately. "I've got a few things to do in the morning, but I reckon I can slip away by lunchtime. How about you and I go out for a few hours and do a pub crawl. I want you to show me who's who in the zoo and how you spot the players. I need to know what I'm looking for. You said Maria was into this too, so she can join us and it'll not fuck up your holiday."

"Nup, she won't come with us. If she's conscious she'll hang out at the pool, but she's got a heap of mates up here, she won't get lonely. But Kat, you're over-complicating this mate. I'm happy to hold up the bar with ya but moving the gear is really fucking easy."

"Then fucking show me."

Next day I half lifted my hand to knock on the flywire door of the unit, but he was already standing there. He pushed the door open.

"Come in, I want to show you something," he said without any formalities, waving his arm in the general direction of the open plan living area.

He was dressed rough as guts, like every other bloke in Broome was on a hot Saturday afternoon; thongs, jeans with the legs cut out and a black T-shirt with the faded logo of some rock band I'd never heard of.

On the dining table was a baseball cap, two coffee mugs and an open newspaper spread out like a cheap-shit tablecloth. He delicately lifted the newspaper, exposing 14 postage stamp sized zip-top bags and one larger bag, all with white powder in them.

"What the fu—" I started to say but he cut me off.

"I've split this up and halved it. So, this is half an ounce and, like I explained last night, you'd get fourteen smaller bags at a gram each, well nearly a gram, I've saved a bit for 'Ron', if you know what I mean?"

I got the drift okay, he was skimming off the top for *'later-on'*.

He continued, "Not sure how good my luck is so we'll leave the half ounce here and just take the gram bags with us."

"How much you selling them for?"

"I told you yesterday, one-twenty. But I've already made dough by making them point nine per bag not the full gram. Dickheads buying a gram don't own scales. Point nine and a gram look the same, they won't pick it."

"Fuck me. You're onto it hey?" I said as I tried to keep up with the shifty side tricks of the trade.

He disappeared off into the bedroom with what I had by then calculated was a bag weighing 15.4 grams and stashed it somewhere I didn't need to know about.

When he walked back out he stuffed the 14 bags into one pocket, took a final swig of cold coffee and declared, "Let's go. Where you taking me?"

"I figured we'd start in town, do a bit of a loop and finish back here."

"Relax, Kat. You're strung up like a fucking Startovarious violin. It ain't that hard mate, I'll show ya."

I decided not to correct his classical music knowledge or his butchering of a long dead Italian's name, but instead followed him outside for my first drug run. As a bit of an afterthought, I asked, "Where's your missus?"

"Fucked if I know, gone out with a couple of her skanky mates."

I made a tactical blunder by taking him to the best pub in town first, part of the learning curve at my expense. We walked out onto the manicured lawn of the beer garden, well-dressed patrons sprinkled around the place, fluted glasses in the hands of the women.

Pablo was turning his head inside out, looking around. "Where's the main bar?" he asked.

"You're standing in it."

"What's inside?"

"Function rooms."

"Then we're in the wrong joint. The only thing happening here today is likely me getting arrested. What's next on your list?"

As we walked back to my car, I realised I'd fucked up by taking him somewhere with a bit of decorum. That wasn't the clientele he was looking for. So I changed tack and we headed to the roughest pub in town. A place that would probably have his black T-shirt ripped off his back in the first ten minutes.

"Now we're cooking with gas," he said as we walked into the beer garden. Scruffily dressed individuals, unshaven, uncouth, raised voices and that was just the women, sat, stood and stumbled around the concrete floored 'garden'. A distinct combination of body odour and stale beer melted the nose hairs as we got closer to the bar.

Pablo followed me into the place because he'd never been there before and I knew where I was going. "I'll get the first round, you find a seat."

When I'd returned with the two pints, he had found a concrete table complimented with a concrete seat and had his back against the wall facing the fest pit of fuckheads and tortured souls you'd never invite home for a Sunday roast for fear they would carve their initials into your mother's dining room table, or indeed, your mother.

"Here," he said, pointing to the space beside him. "Sit here so you can see what's going on." His eyes were darting all over the place. "Mate I've been into some rough joints in my life, but this takes the cake. What's with all the concrete tables and chairs?"

I laughed. "Welcome to Broome. It's so it can't be thrown around in a fight."

"You serious?"

"Yep, true story."

He hadn't taken one sip out of his beer when he says, "Stay here and keep your eyes open."

"Where—" but I didn't get to finish as he'd stood up and was headed for the 'Men's'.

Four or five minutes passed before he walked out closely followed by a skinny bloke in his mid-30's wearing what would originally have been a quality light blue collared shirt but now had the sleeves cut out and a rich red pindan tinge through it. The two of them exchanged a couple of words, Pablo walked back to our table and the skinny bloke shambled off in the opposite direction.

"Okay," he says, sitting back down and reaching for his beer. "The words out that I've got a few grams on me. Ole' mate's eyes lit up like saucers when I dropped it on him. Don't stare too hard but he's doing the rounds with that group he's with at the pool table.

Pablo never got to finish the beer I bought him. Over the next 25 minutes he had four different punters and one of the barmen give him a nod, followed by a conference in the toilet.

"We're out of here, Kat."

"That's it?" I asked, bewildered at what had just unfolded. The learning curve of the drug trade was steep.

On the drive back to his accommodation, he filled in the finer details at the same time as he pulled cash out from different pockets of his remodelled shorts.

"We went in with 14 grams, sold 10, came out with 4 and… let me count this… 950 bucks. The barman wanted an eight-ball but I wasn't going to be fucked around sorting that out and sold him 4 bags for three-fiddy, plus the six single sales is $950."

I had no idea what he was talking about. "What the fuck is an eight-ball?"

"An eighth of an ounce, 3.5 grams. You'd sell it at a discounted rate because the loser is big noting himself and buying a larger quantity in one hit. I wasn't going to sit in that cubicle trying to juggle the shit on my knee sorting out 3.5 grams, so I cut him a deal and sold him 4 bags that were only .9 anyway. Everyone's a winner mate." He continued to juggle the fistful of dollars. "I need a fucking calculator. At a 1000 bucks an ounce, a gram is worth about 35. We just sold a total of 9. Nine by 35 is what?"

"Three hundred fifteen," I said quickly. Pablo gave me a sideways stare. "What can I say, I've always been good at maths."

He nodded. "I'm impressed. Okay, so take 315 off 950, what's that?"

"Six thirty-five."

"That's profit Kat. Six hundred and thirty-five fucking drinking vouchers in however long we were there. I buy it at a bit less than what you'd be paying but you get the idea. Those clowns think we've left to go get more because the whole joint knows it's available and wants in but we're not going back. They don't need to see my head again. Here, put some fuel in your car," he said as he poked a grey hundred-dollar bill into the ashtray.

"Kind of you mate, thanks."

"Now listen to me Kat, I'm as serious as a fucking heart attack. If you're going to have a crack at this, be smart mate. There's a good quid in the game for those with something between their ears. Don't ever try to do what I did today, I was only showing you how it works at the bottom end of the food chain and it's a fucking jungle. Find someone who's smarter and a bit more switched on than those yo-yo's today. Sell it in bulk, double your dough, put the price up, put a Broome surcharge on it, they'll pay it, then stand back and watch them do all the hard sell and take the risks. It's not your style mate to be wandering around the concrete tables selling fucking dope."

"No. It's not," I agreed, but had to ask the obvious question, "Where do you get the shit from?"

"You're never going to know that mate. Otherwise, I'd be chopping myself out. I buy in at about half what you'll pay but I get a bucket full at a time mate and you won't be going there because I won't let it happen. If you know the right doors to knock on, most of it comes out of Sydney or Melbourne."

He wasn't giving too much away there.

"You ever been in the slammer, Kat?"

"Why?"

"Because if you get caught dealing ounces, you will. Make no fucking mistake about that mate."

"Yeah, three months in Fremantle in the late 70's. 'B division'."

"Bullshit. You serious? B division was non-conformists, right?"

"It was. But I'm yanking your chain, I was working there, not an inmate."

"Doing what?"

"Replacing the wire-mesh opening between levels that got trashed during a riot. Fuckers had been using it as trampolines." I laughed with him. "I was working three levels up on a scaffold by myself one day and a shit head walked underneath me with only a pair of shorts on. Welding sparks ran down his neck and he gave me a blast, so I told him to go fuck himself. He started climbing up the ladders on the inside of the scaffold, telling the whole prison he was going to throw me off. I shit me'self.

When he poked his head up through the trap door, I kicked it closed as hard as I could on his fuckin' head. Cunt fell back down two levels."

"How did ya get out of that alive?"

"Wasn't easy. Guards came from everywhere, Claxton went off and they escorted me straight out the front gate. I wasn't allowed back in 'cos they couldn't guarantee my welfare."

"Well, Freo's closed now but you'll get a holiday somewhere if you get caught. If you get done don't bother taking me with you hey." It was more a statement than a question.

I walked out of his holiday unit two hours later with an ounce of upper in one pocket and a set of scales in the other at the mate's rate of $1000 and drove straight to the Dodger's house.

Wife number two opened the flywire door to let me in. She hated my guts because Dodger spent more time with me than her and she could only offer a grunt and a wave of her hand towards the back of the house and the sun deck.

It was none of my business and I wasn't going to bring the subject up with him, but I couldn't get my head around why they were together. She had the personality of a fucking lamppost and they fought like cat and dog. Dodger had told me once that when they first met, she could suck a golf ball through a garden hose. The thought made the hair on the back of my neck stand up as I walked past her and into the house.

She didn't have it in her to sit out the back with us to chat or lower herself to offer a coffee or God forbid, a beer. So, I had Dodger to myself.

I gave him a full run-down on my meeting with Pablo the night before and the crash course in drugs and fuckwits at the pub a few hours earlier. To my surprise, he knew less than I did about the subject. He knew a bit about weed, I reckon that came from firsthand experience, but nothing about this gear.

After a pause, he offered, "Okay, I think we might know someone who could be our middleman."

"You do?"

"We do. Let's go find, TC."

TC

If you ever wanted a reason for loving Broome, try this on.

A stinking hot night.

Cold beer.

Standing at an open-air bar on the edge of the desert, waves crashing on Cable Beach a hundred metres away to the west.

More cold beer.

A live Paul Kelly concert in front of you and it's going off.

Even more cold beer.

The Dodger and I went to every Paul Kelly concert held in Broome, we knew every word of every song and the atmosphere and ambiance was about as Australian as you could ever get.

We liked Paul Kelly but to be fair most of the town turned up to any concert, because we liked anyone who came to Broome for our entertainment, regardless of who they were. This night we had parked ourselves down the back against the bar and were playing up like a couple of sixteen-year old's who had jumped the fence at their first gig.

Two Cougars on holiday from Melbourne were doing their best to get into our pants. They were pouring jugs of beer into us at a ferocious rate in the hope our eyesight might wane and we would take them on. We played the game for most of the night, dancing with them, throwing them around, spilling beer everywhere and singing as loud and as boisterous as we could get away with without getting thrown out, but throughout it all we kept our eyes on the real prize.

At an interval when the noise wasn't quite so loud, we slipped away to the inside of the pub and positioned ourselves in the eye

line of a fiery little bullshit artist we called TC. A few months beforehand he'd worked for us for a week but had been a bit too casual
for our liking, so we'd given him the flick. He left our yard with a
week's wages in cash and a new nickname. He'd been happy enough
with his new moniker until he discovered from one of his mates that
it didn't stand for Top Cat. Apparently after introducing himself as,
'just call me TC' his drinking buddy had announced, "You know
Dodger called you that because he thought you were a little Tasmanian Cunt?"

Since which, every time he saw us, especially when he had a gut's
full of amber courage, he'd storm over loaded to the eyeballs and
give us a mouthful. You could set your watch by his reaction and
that's what we were depending on during this concert.

Despite him being all bullshit and bluster, he had an unusual physique with quite wide shoulders for his size. It made him look like
he'd been doing two hundred push-ups a day since he was four years
old. Added to that was how he walked, or more properly, swaggered;
he'd move his shoulders forward, left and right, like he was carrying
a full suitcase in either hand. If you didn't know him, he could easily
have come across as a bit intimidating, but we had history with him
so we were more threatened by a Jägermeister chaser than his loud
voice and arm waving antics.

Still, here he was, poking Dodger in the chest, extremely indignant at our collective Christening of him, demanding an apology for
the umpteenth time and insisting we not call him it again. We did
what we usually did and laughed at him.

It was a big call on his behalf to be taking us both on like this
and interrupting our Paul Kelly concert. Even if we had wanted him
to, he didn't know that, yet.

At full volume, Dodger and I discussed taking a leg and an arm
each and throwing him over the back fence. He wasn't a heavy
weight bloke, the prick would have been lucky to weigh 70 kilos so
we figured it was achievable.

We made out that the delay was our uncertainty in whether his body would clear the barbed wire strands along the top or if he'd get tangled up in it.

One of the security blokes that we were lucky to know, a massive Māori bloke about four-foot wide, came over and suggested we bring it down a bit. At a small nod from Dodger, that had cost us fifty bucks to arrange, our Māori friend escorted me, Dodge and TC off the premises.

Outside the pub on a near empty road and away from all the prying eyes we pinned TC against a wall.

Dodger had a pretty solid belief that TC was into a bit of speed and now we were going to find out.

"Oi, shut the fuck up with the noise and attitude and fuckin' listen."

Almost in a sulk, TC said, "What?"

***

An hour and a half later TC rocked up to my place and threw two grand on the table.

"You serious?" I asked. "Where the fuck you get that from?"

"What do you care?"

I figured with a quick glance over to Dodger, we didn't.

"You want the whole ounce, in one hit?"

"Yep. And I'll be back for another one."

"This ounce," I said, sliding it across the table in front of him, "is less the sample we gave you, 27.1." I had to tell him this in case he had scales. Turns out he did.

"It better be the same as the fucking sample," he snarled.

"It is. Now I'm telling you for the last time, drop the fucking attitude before I drop you."

"Just one thing…" he said, his tone easing a little.

"What?" Dodger and I said in unison.

"My name's Jeremy."

He took the reduced ounce and we told him to have a good night.

25

And, that's how it started.

I saw Pablo again the next morning, before he flew out. Bought another ounce and a few dregs that he just happened to have on him and placed an order for four more ounces that he would freight up in the next few days. We sorted out some details about transport, payment and communication methods.

He gave me a bit of a lecture around using mobile phones. It really wasn't a big deal though, getting a signal on my mobile was a hit and miss thing up here, so landlines were still the main way to call someone.

Pablo's paranoia wasn't assuaged and he stressed that the cops had the potential to listen in. So, we spent a bit of time setting up a system using other people's landlines that would suffice for the immediate future.

The one principle was that I would be his contact. No one else. Dodger was to handle TC, I didn't want or need to have anything to do with that dickhead. He was too much of a loose cannon for my liking. However, credit where it was due, it became obvious over the next few months that he was connected to the Broome underbelly well enough to move the gear fast. He made a decent dollar in the process. I had no doubt some of his proceeds were going into his own arm or up his nose or being stirred into his morning coffee, none of which affected my life in any way.

The shifty prick was into everything. During the week when he'd worked for us, he'd sold Dodger a sawn-off, single-barrel shotgun with a plastic bag full of shells for a hundred bucks.

When Dodger showed me, I told him to get rid of it. There was no way of knowing how many bank tellers had looked down the end of it or who'd pulled the trigger on who.

"Take it out of town twenty k's and run the shells through it if that's what turns you on, then get rid of it. My best advice would be not to fire it one handed with a solid round in the barrel, or you'll break your wrist."

That whole shotgun thing had always put me on edge about TC so me and Dodger had set up some firm ground rules with him. All deals in cash, we weren't a bank so 'don't ask' for credit was how business was done. Surprisingly, for me anyway, with those rules in place, he wasn't a difficult bloke to do business with apart from the fact he looked like and smelt like a hobo. But he had the cash up front, often handing Dodger a shoebox or a plastic bag at their designated handover point in the top carpark out at Gantheaume Point. In the bag or box would be an unstacked pile of notes made up of every denomination. It always counted correct, but it was a scruffy way to do business.

The Dodger met him at his flat once. TC rolled up the lounge carpet and there were notes everywhere, thousands of dollars spread between the carpet and the underlay. Dodger had to help him count it out on the lounge room floor.

After about a month, TC had upped his weekly order to six ounces which indicated that he was selling it in bulk to someone else who we wished we had found first.

***

On Australia Day, 1993 that top carpark out at Gantheaume Point was playing host to a packed sausage sizzle, so rather than doing a drug deal in the mist of 2,000 Broome families, Dodger and TC changed the drop-off point to be a location in China Town.

I had a bit of time up my sleeve, so I decided to go for a ride with Dodger and see what was going on, however we had a small problem. The previous Friday, we had allowed a builder to unload a semi full of his gear in our yard, kitchen cabinets and other top-end furniture that had to be hand unloaded. The guy wouldn't be back until after the Australia Day weekend and rather than shuffling the semi around, which was blocking our own cars, he just lent us his brand new Hilux for a couple of days. It meant using someone else's car for a drug drop and I wasn't thrilled with the idea, but I thought, what could go wrong? Plenty, turns out.

I jumped into the driver's seat and Dodger got in the passenger side with a backpack.

We were halfway into town when he pulled out that fucking sawn-off shotgun from the bag and put it on the floor.

"You're fucking kidding me! I told you to get rid of it. What's it doing in the car? Are we going to rob a bank? You picked the wrong day you fucking dill, their all shut. And anyway, I'm not playing fucking Bonnie to your Clyde."

Dodge waved his hand to calm me down. "It's only so TC knows I still have it."

"Why, he sold it to you remember? You going to shoot him in the main street?"

"I just want to keep him on his toes."

"Fucking terrific. Why not fire at him, see if he'll dance on his toes for you… for fuck's sake Dodge," I said glaring across at him.

I swung into Napier Terrace with Male Oval on my left. What I didn't see until it was too late was an indigenous, middle-aged man, drunk as a skunk, balancing with his toes hanging over the curb. Good thing I wasn't going very quick as the instant I got to him he fell face first into the front of the Hilux. There was a distinct thump as he disappeared under the car. I stamped on the brakes.

My first thought was, I'm fucked. Quickly followed by, we're fucked.

I'm driving someone else's car.

I've just killed someone.

There's six ounces of amphetamine in a backpack on the floor.

There's a sawn-off shotgun in the footwell.

I couldn't remember any other occasion in my life where I'd been so unglued with fear.

I hadn't moved, my hands still wrapped around the steering wheel and staring straight ahead when Dodger got out of the car. Clearly, he hadn't gripped the severity of the situation like I had, or he was better at dealing with life changing fuckups.

To my amazement a hand, followed by an arm appeared and the gentleman I'd just run over slid out from under the passenger side of the car. Dodger lifted the bloke up to his feet and the guy started laughing.

"You fucking missed me that time, ya white cunt," he said in his best Kimberley accent.

Without so much as a flinch, Dodger replied, "No we didn't," and punched the bloke square on the nose. As the old fella fell back onto the oval, Dodger jumped back in the car and like a bad impression of some US TV cop show shouted, "Let's go."

I had to be dreaming this.

I let my foot off the brake and we rolled away like it was just another day in Broome.

My heart was still racing and we hadn't said a word as we cruised up through China Town.

We both spotted TC at the same time from a hundred metres off. He was pacing up and down the side of his car, crouching, standing, crouching, standing, like a fucking Meerkat.

He was off his head.

If he was trying to look inconspicuous, then a neon sign announcing, 'Drug Deal Here!' might have looked less obvious.

We pulled up behind him and he launched himself at Dodger's side window, throwing a supermarket plastic bag full of cash into Dodger's lap.

"There's 10K, where's my gear?"

"I haven't got time to sit here and count this, if it's a dollar short I'll be looking for you," Dodger said as he handed the backpack out through the window with the shotgun visible in his lap.

The backpack could have been empty, the Meerkat didn't even look inside.

He danced across the road like a drunk on roller skates and stopped out the front of a business where two tall, heavily built fuckers with tatts all over them were standing. It was blatantly obvious they were waiting on TC.

As we drove off everyone eyeballed each other and Dodger gave them a royal wave like the Queen driving past her devoted people. No one smiled.

We needed to get out of the area fast. If someone had seen the debacle with the indigenous guy and reported the car rego, then the cops might be looking for us. And now, added to the shotgun, we also had $10k of unexplained cash in the car.

I drove out past the back of the police station and the Mangrove Hotel, avoiding the oval where another sausage sizzle was taking place in front of the Tourist Bureau. When we got to our yard, I drove straight past, heading towards the wharf.

"Where we going?" asked Dodger.

"We have a few things to sort out. Firstly, if we're going to continue with our new trade, we need to be a hell of a lot smarter and more streetwise than what just went down then, or we might as well go to the police station and hand ourselves in now."

"You ran the bloke over."

"I'm not fucking talking about that," I shouted. "That's the least of our problems. I'll tell you how this is going to unfold. You're gunna give TC the arse, he's a nut case and I don't trust him. Those two pricks with the tatts have seen us. They know who TC is getting the whippa from now and we know he's on-selling it to them."

Dodge tried to interrupt me, but I cut him off. "We know who they are and where they work. So we go and have a meeting with them. We tell them we're cutting TC out and are happy to deal with them directly."

"But if TC finds out he'll go fuckin' ballistic. He'll be way worse than spitting the dummy over his nickname."

"Exactly. That's why we'll tell him we've run out or our supplier got done, tell him any fucking thing you want but we drop him. He can start buying his personnel requirements off the tatt blokes if he wants. We need to find people higher up the food chain than TC and we deal in bulk, golden rule number one, we don't go near the bottom feeders. TC's too close to the street." I took a breath but couldn't resist one last dig. "And doing a handover in the main street was a really fucking stupid idea." I finished my rant as we were driving past the coffee shop-café at the entrance to the wharf.

"Yeah, fair enough. But it was still you that ran the bloke over, ya dumb cunt," Dodger said and mock-punched me on the shoulder with a laugh. As he looked back out of the car we had reached the wharf and the rattle of the timber planks shook the vehicle. "What exactly are we doing here? You going to drive us off the end of the pier, Louise?"

"I fucking should, but no, Thelma, just one more tidy up," I said and continued to drive out to the end where two old blokes were fishing. There was no one else in sight. I did a U-turn and came back about halfway. Dodger was looking at me waiting for an explanation. I pulled up and pointed to the shotgun. "You throw it, or I throw it."

"Fuck you, Kat. No fucking way. No. It's okay for you, how many do you own? Two? Three? Fuck off!"

He had a soft point, but it was a big stretch. I was a member of the Broome Pistol Club and would often go out there on a Tuesday night when they had club nights and put a few rounds down the range using two .22 calibre target pistols that I owned. The big difference that he failed to acknowledge was that the guns were legal and licensed to me, but I wasn't licensed to remove them from the club secretary's control. I had nowhere to store them properly, so I'd never applied for that part of the licence. And I certainly wasn't driving around town with handguns sitting on the front seat.

A couple of years later I would purchase a Remington .223 semi-automatic rifle from one of the club members and extended my licence to allow me to store all my firearms in a gun safe installed at my house. A month after I bought the Remington, a lunatic went on a rampage in Port Arthur, Tasmania and the Australian gun laws tightened severely. I handed it in with no hesitation as it was one of the few laws I agreed with and the government buy-back scheme was fair. I picked up a grand more than I had paid for it. But that was all in the future. The sawn-off was more immediate.

"Give me the fucking gun. We're not gangsters or hit men, Dodger. We're trying really hard to be accepted as solid citizens running a decent business. We do not need to be caught with that on us. It'll draw attention that we don't need." I turned in my seat to look at him. "Besides, someone will get hurt."

"It isn't loaded," he said, in a voice that reminded me of a little kid sulking.

I tried hard not to laugh. "Fuck me drunk, are you serious? You took a gun to a drug deal expecting some sort of trouble and it's not even loaded? Get real. You basically brought a stick to a gunfight? Where are the shells you had for it?"

"I ran them through it, like you said. None left. Can you get me some more?"

"Fuck off. That ain't going to happen. Stop stalling and turf it."

He got out of the car like the still sulky, spoilt kid. He looked up and down the pier to check no one was watching, walked over to the edge, kissed the barrel like the bloke on TV kisses his fish catch and threw it as far as he could into Roebuck Bay.

He wasn't happy but I knew he'd get over it.

On the way back into the yard we discussed the small issue of running over the bloke in town.

"If anyone saw what happened and got the rego number the cops will trace it."

"Yeah," Dodger agreed, "but Bazza said we could borrow it."

"True, but if the Jacks do come knocking, we stick to the story that the bloke fell in front of the car. When we stopped, he didn't appear hurt, you picked him up and sat him back down in the park. He was as drunk as a thousand men, he told you he was okay and to fuck off, so we left."

"Do we say he fell on his face to explain the nose I gave him?" Dodger asked.

"We just say he must've hit it when he went under the car."

As it was, no one came calling. The local police didn't give a shit for an old drunk indigenous guy who may, or may not, have been assaulted in the street. That was just too much of a daily occurrence to get wound up about.

Bill & Ben, The Flowerpot Men

Both tattooed blokes had a very high opinion of themselves.

The image they wanted to present to the rest of the world was that they were big tough bikies, running with a gang, afraid of no one, oblivious to the law and the louder their motorbike was the more you had to piss your pants when they went by.

In truth, they were no more connected to the real bikey gangs of Western Australia than my mum was. Had they been, I doubt I'd have gone near them and even Dodger would have been wary. These two were wannabes.

We cold-called on them with no forewarning that we were dropping in for a chat. As we walked in the door of their piss-ant business they jumped up and pushed their chests out. Folded arms, stretched necks, jutted chins, they were trying to posture like two fighting cocks. All they looked like were cocks. Thinking their tattooed sleeves would terrify the fuck out of us.

Wankers.

No one introduced themselves. This wasn't tea and cakes on a Sunday. Wankers or not, this was still a serious business and we had to establish who was in charge. Dodger took the lead. That man had the eloquence of a politician some days.

"Right you cunts, fucking listen to me, I'm only going to say this once. We might have a business proposal for you, but it won't involve that Tasmanian Cunt."

"We're listening," the one with the Tā moko on his chin said.

Dodger laid it out exactly as we had discussed. Bottom line was, "Are you interested, how much do you want and when?"

"Yeah, okay and we'll start with six ounces as soon as you can, on credit till we take more."

Dodger, turned around and started to walk out the front door, saying to me, "Let's go. These pricks think we're a fuckin' bank."

Almost in unison, the pair dropped the tough guy facade, "Woah, hang on, what's the problem?"

Dodger was playing them big time and I knew it. "You used the 'C-word'. We don't do credit, not for anyone for any reason. Cash on delivery or fuck off."

"Okay, okay, settle down. What about quality?"

"Whatever you brought off TC out the front of here last week is what it is. You took it straight off him, so he hadn't the chance to cut it. What you got then is what you'll get from now on. We don't clip the ticket with icing sugar or brick dust on the way past. We had no control over what TC did with it before you guys got hold of it previously."

"Fair enough. And weights?"

"Our weights, like our quality, will be spot on."

Now Dodger was yanking the bloke's chain on that, we may have had control over the weights, but we were totally reliant on Pablo staying true to his word that the product was good quality on arrival to us. If he decided to dud us on $20 or $30k and sent us bags of sugar, we were rooted.

The one thing that didn't add up with these two was their bragging about how well they were connected to a couple of unsavoury groups around Australia. I knew that if they had been that well connected, they'd have been selling the gear to us, instead of buying it from us. Maybe it fooled the rest of the town and got them some kudos. For me and Dodger, they were bullshit artists.

As we went to leave, one of them held out his hand as a peace offering to shake on the deal. Now this is a big boy game where the tough bloke squeezes the others hand as a show of physical strength and in his own mind, strength of character. Well, I was one palm flinch ahead of him on this little trick, so we crunched hands at full force and I held it rock solid for five seconds.

The combined pressure would have burst a can of beer.

"We have a deal, Kat," he said, trying to hold eye contact.

Back in our car I asked Dodger, "What are their names?"

"Wouldn't have a clue, they didn't say. Let's christen them Bill and Ben."

"The Flowerpot Men," I said and laughed.

"What?" Dodger looked blank at the reference.

"Never mind," I said and then paused a beat. "We didn't tell them ours, did we?"

"No."

"Then how did the fucker know my name?"

Except he didn't of course. My given name was something I hadn't been called by anyone, friends or family, for a long, long time. The nickname, "Kat", had been with me for as long as I could remember.

My French-born mother would tell me that the first words I ever spoke were, '*Mon Chat*' so for a short period of time she would call me, Mon Chat as a term of endearment. No different than calling a kid, 'Sweetie', 'Bub' or 'Flower'. It was warm, it was kind, it was loving. But it was also French.

My father had cottoned on to the phrase and fully understood my dear mother's affectionate terminology, but living in Australia, it translated badly. Mon Chat in French translates as 'My Cat'. An Australian attempting to speak French would likely pronounce Chat as 'Shat' and that meant a completely different thing. My mother was horrified to learn this little piece of Aussie slang and the thought that her Australian friends would think she was calling her first born, 'My shit' wasn't endearing. But she wasn't fazed.

She simplified and Australianised her pet name for me, her only child, so that it progressed from, *Mon Chat* to My Cat and finally 'Kat' with a 'K'. And there it stayed.

In the privacy of our own home, I would remain Mon Chat but in the company of others I was Kat. I do still have a real name, but sometimes I wonder if I even remember it myself. Dodger, of course, as my best mate, had another nickname for me that he would occasionally use. Starting with a 'C' and having four letters, it was best not used in open company.

As per our agreement, Dodger went back around to see Bill and Ben the following morning to drop off the six ounces. Approaching their premises, he noticed a solid looking indigenous bloke passed out on the footpath. The guy had his back against the shopfront wall and was slumped over with his chin in his chest. Even with a gut's full of white wine in him, he must have been uncomfortable.

Ben (who we later decided had the chin tattoo) opened the door to let Dodger in. They swapped the gear for the cash and walked back out the front door together. The transaction had taken less than a minute, was done off the street and to any casual observer would have been hard to spot.

Pointing to the indigenous guy, Dodger said, "You checked his pulse recently?"

"No. Do I look like a fucking doctor?" replied Ben. "He's a regular, sleeps here about twice a week. The sun'll be on him soon, he'll wake up and ask us for a beer. We'll give him a bottle of water, or a can of coke and he'll wander back up to Kennedy Hill and get on the piss again."

"You sure he's okay?" Dodger asked whilst giving in to his own medical training and delivering a not so gentle tap on the guy's bum with his boot. "Hey, wake up. You okay?"

No movement.

Dodger picked up the guy's arm and immediately recognised the feeling of cold that only came with death. He had no clue how long it took for rigor mortis to set in, but the arm was already beginning to stiffen. He gently lowered the arm back into the bloke's lap and straightened up. "I'm out of here. You know where to find us when you want more gear, but you might want to ring someone about your mate here. He's been dead for hours."

"What? You're fucking kidding aren't ya?"

"Which part of 'he's dead' are you struggling with? He's fuckin' dead mate."

"Fuck me. What do I do now?" Ben asked in a panic.

"You wait till I get out of the street then ring someone. Or tell the shop next door to sort it. The guy's leaning against their wall, their problem I guess."

***

Even though we had cut TC out of the mix, he kept coming around. The guy was a magnet for trouble and sure enough it found him.

In the April of '93 he turned up in our yard one afternoon with another bottom feeder in the passenger seat who was twitching that bad I thought he was trying to chew his own ears off. I saw them pull up and set Dodger loose on them, "Get 'em out of here."

They were frantic to get their hands on some gear and sounded Dodger out about where they could get some.

"Wouldn't have a clue mate. I told you we're out of the trade. What about your mates in town, they got any?" Dodger asked, with an innocence that surprised even me.

"We had a blue, I can't go around there."

"Sorry, TC. Can't help you mate. If I hear anything I'll let you know."

"Don't call me TC."

As the car was pulling away, Dodger called out. "See ya, Stilla."

I joined him in the yard. "Stilla?"

"Yeah. Stilla Tasmanian Cunt."

A couple of weeks later we saw Bill and Ben at the local tavern and asked if TC had squared up with them.

"Shithead owed us $2k for ten days, making all sorts of excuses. He's cooked big time, using more than he's selling. We're tossing up about who's gonna take him for a ride out of town and chop his head off with an axe," said Bill.

"I'll lend you the axe," I said, laughing and fairly certain neither Bill nor Ben would have the balls for that shit.

Thing was, the working relationship between Bill, Ben and TC progressively deteriorated due mostly to TC's personal use and his unpredictable nature.

Despite the previous experience of him owing them money, we learnt they'd given him credit a few more times and every time they'd had to chase him down. It beggared belief that they backed themselves into a corner by allowing TC credit once, let alone on repeat occasions. I figured, given his demeanour, no one would have loaned him so much as a ten-cent piece, but Bill and Ben must have had more charity in their hearts. And a lot more patience, yet I couldn't help wondering where it might end up.

The big problem TC had was that the wannabe biker-boys were the only ones he could get gear from, he had no other supplier, so was forced to crawl back to them with cap in hand every time he needed a clout. And although they were stupid enough to continue playing the game of boom and bust with him, even they had to have limits.

Their relationship came to a head one day when TC burst into their shop completely off his head, screaming and yelling like a lunatic. Once again, he owed them money but at the top of his voice and talking at one-hundred miles an hour, he told them that the product was only sugar, they'd jumped on it and they could write their dough off because they were only thieving cunts anyway.

The best he was going to offer them was that they cancel the debt and start afresh there and then. He told them that they needed to drop half an ounce on him and he'd bring the dough back to them in a day or two.

They told him to fuck off.

A couple of punches were thrown and TC was manhandled into the street.

Ten minutes later TC made a seriously bad decision, in a no doubt miserable life that had been filled with them.

He re-entered the shop with a truck load of attitude in him. Louder and more aggressive, overheard by a few people out in the street, TC shouted that he was prepared to take them both on.

"I'll rip your fucking heads off."

"Fuck off, TC."

"If you pricks won't sort me out I'm going straight to the cops. They'll deal me. They'll deal me for free. I tells them what youse pricks are up to and they'll deal me all I fuckin' want!"

From what I heard later, most punters walked straight on by. Shouting and arguing was fairly normal given some of the characters that used to hang around that end of town. But one listener told me TC continued his rant by suggesting that if 'they' weren't prepared to pull half an ounce out of their pockets immediately his next stop would be to Hamersley Street and the front door of the cop shop.

I was smiling as I was being told all this, but the smile froze when I heard what TC had ended his tirade with.

"I'll give the Jacks a full run-down on you two fuck heads and while I'm there I'll lag in your fucking mates, Dodger and that Cool Cat cunt. You know the coppers will love me for that right? That's how they work. I'll have them eating out of my hands, you watch."

Two days later, while launching his dingy off the back of its trailer on the low tide at Gantheaume Point, a grey nomad spotted the roof of TC's Datsun poking through the waves and reported it to the police.

Transportation

By late May '93 we were really kicking a few goals.

Bill and Ben had been on board for a few months and despite my initial reservations, they were doing exceptionally well. It had only taken them half that time to triple their weekly order and as the months progressed they'd continue to take more and were flawless to work with.

After we all got over our huffing and puffing and putting on the act of who was the toughest and who had the biggest dick, our relationship improved no end.

They came across as reasonable blokes that we could share a laugh and a beer with, although we kept the social side to an absolute minimum so that an outsider didn't conclude that we were business partners in any sense.

We had to be a bit inventive in how we exchanged powder for cash each Friday and had educated them into wearing long-sleeve work shirts and driving discreet cars instead of sporting black sleeveless shirts and floating around on motorbikes with exhaust systems that would wake the dead.

The Dodger had been busy sourcing other players in town and was good at it. The rest weren't in the same league as Bill and Ben but two ounces here, four there, an odd one or two somewhere else and we found ourselves turning over a pound to a pound and a half a week in no time.

My role was to keep getting the product into Broome undetected and the cash back to Perth. Easy when we were doing ounces. Bit more thought required when we were shifting pounds of the stuff.

My relationship with Pablo was built on trust, he was making a big quid out of us and we were making a living because of him, so neither of us was going to shaft the other. The business was just too good to fuck up and trust had to be factored into the equation.

We had established a fairly good communication system whereby I would ring him twice a week. I'd use the phone box opposite the Continental Hotel at 9:00 in the morning every Monday and Friday, dialling a Perth number that belonged to his elderly grandmother who lived a street away from him. Pablo picked up on the first ring, knowing it was going to be me. I'm sure he had others on the go but that was my time slot.

In the early start-up stage, when I was only ordering up to four ounces a week, he would wrap it up in old clothing or a towel and put it into a padded Australia Post bag. The address on the front would be my post office box number but the name would be anything Pablo could think of. I'd send the cash back to his grandmother's house the same way.

As the quantities and the value increased, we had to consider other alternatives. Working with a weekly ordering and payment system was stressful and increasing the chances of coming unstuck so we moved to larger quantities that would carry us for three to four weeks at a time.

The obvious answer was to use road freight, but you couldn't just pack up a box labelled, 'Drugs. For the use of…'

We had to be inventive and the main downside was that it took a bit longer to get to Broome, but the weight could be hidden better and in ever-increasing amounts. The first cover-story Pablo came up with was to buy four mag wheels off the wreckers, removing one or more of the tires, putting the well wrapped bags of amphetamine inside the tire and back onto the rim, resealing it and putting pressure back in. The wheels would be stacked onto a pallet four high, wrapped in plastic and strapped down using nylon strap and clips. A printed sticker on the front would read, "Hold in yard for collection" and bore a dodgy name on it that only I would know.

I'd do the same with the cash, rewrapping the wheels exactly as they were, taking them back to the same transport yard and telling them they were going back to Perth because they were the wrong stud centres. Giving the courier company instructions that someone would pick them up from the yard at the other end. We did this a few times, changing freight companies on each occasion so a trucking depot wouldn't spot the same scam twice. When we thought we had run our luck with the mag wheels we changed to second-hand fridges that Pablo brought in Cannington, Perth from a company that sold old and new appliances.

Sending rusty old and knackered fridges up to Broome was of course a recipe for disaster. Even the slowest of cops would have asked what the fuck was going on with that. But the eye sees what it wants to see. So… what Pablo did was to buy said rusty old fridge and then grab a new cardboard box from the industrial waste bins out the back of the company's unit. Slip it over the old fridge, add some tie wraps in the right pace and a sheaf of official looking receipts. One new fridge on its way to the tropical north where, let's face it, we needed all the fucking fridges we could get our hands on. I mean, how else do you get cold beer?

Never one to lose out on a deal, Dodger used to make a couple of extra dollars by actually selling the second-hand fridges. Without the contents, of course.

Several times Pablo sent his wife, Maria, to Broome for a short holiday with her friends, which eased the stress of transporting tens of thousands of dollars in cash by road.

But I had a few problems with that.

At one point we owed him forty grand, plus I was going to drop another forty on the table for the next order.

Eighty grand is a lot of dough to be hiding down the front of her bra, even if she was amply stacked, so I needed to talk to her on her arrival at Broome airport. When she got off the plane, sashaying towards the exit concourse with a skirt nearer her navel than the bottom of her arse, there was more than a hint of surprise when she spotted me.

With an expression like a teenager caught smoking behind a bike shed, she blurted out, "Hi, what are you doing here?"

"Arranging some cash for Pablo, where do you want it?"

"Um, I guess…" She looked past me towards the exit door of the airport before returning her attention to my question. "When I fly out on Friday, not now. Plane leaves at two o'clock, I'll meet you here at one. Put it in a bag like this." She held up an open ended bag, the type I'd seen most tourists use for their towels down on the beaches of Broome.

"You sure?"

"I'll put some other shit on top and sit it on my lap."

As an afterthought, she pulled out a kid's plastic sandwich box from her bag. "Nearly forgot, this is for you, a present from Pablo. Eight ounces. He said to sort it out later."

I almost laughed. I wondered how Pablo, who still hated me calling him that name, felt that even his missus used it now.

"Okay, you need a lift?" I asked to cover my snigger.

She was a bit vague, "No… I'm being picked up… um, by a… friend. Thanks anyway. I just, um, need to go to the toilet. See-ya Friday."

I walked out of the terminal, but I sensed some unease that I couldn't quite get a handle on. Broome airport isn't exactly JFK, so sitting in the carpark I could easily see back towards the exit doors. A few minutes later, Maria walked out the door, hand in hand with some bloke I'd never seen before. Tracking them to his car, I watched him open the door for her. Before she got in, he was all over her like a rash. I'm all for being friendly with friends, but I'd never given any casual women friends a quick fingering in a car park.

Maria wasn't hard on the eyes, so I could appreciate his interest in her but clearly, he was not her brother.

I had a big dilemma here. I could not ring Pablo and ask him whose idea it was that his wife come to Broome for a few days? Or if he knew she was doing the Watusi two step with some punter up here?

My way out of it was to wait till our 9:00 am phone hook-up on the Friday, before she flew out and ask him if he was happy I'd be handing her eighty grand? Then the problem wasn't mine.

I took note of the vehicle and rego that they got into and told Dodger to keep his eyes open around town for it.

My concern here was that although Pablo and I had what I thought was a sacrosanct agreement, he wouldn't sell any gear into Broome unless it was through Dodger and me, maybe he had a similar idea to our commitment as Maria had to her marriage vows.

Pablo hadn't said anything to me earlier in the day about the eight ounces in the sandwich box so could the package have been intended for the other bloke and the wife had made a blue by handing it to me? Maybe I was reading too much into all this, or I was becoming paranoid. Probably a bit of both.

Friday's conversation was uneventful. He assured me Maria knew what she was doing and 'thanks for the $80K'.

"Did you get the half pound?" he asked.

"Yeah, no worries, it was a gift hey?"

"No, it was not a fucking gift!"

"Fair enough. Can't hate me for trying. We'll make the adjustment at our next financial meeting. Alright?" I said and we both laughed it off.

He knew I was taking the piss and I decided that telling him about Maria and her friend was not part of my job description.

Later that morning I wrapped the eighty up neat and tight, put it in the bottom of a heavy-duty tourist bag that cost me five bucks and handed it over to her in the terminal. I never sighted the lover.

Now Pablo had agreed to the transfer, I had no stress with her carrying the dough onto the plane. Not only was Broome airport no JFK, but Australia was not Europe with their myriad of home-grown terrorists that had plagued internal flights since the 1970's. A flight from Broome to Perth in the early '90s had no security whatsoever. I'd seen people getting on with esky's full of fish they had caught the day before, ice melting and dripping in a pale red trail down the aisle. Hell, who knew if the esky only had dead fish in it. I always thought it would have been a good way to get rid of a body. Carrying a bit of cash wasn't going to raise any eyebrows.

The Roof Plumber

Not long after TC disappeared, we met the Roof Plumber.

He was, funnily enough, a real roof plumber and as busy as a one-armed paper hanger. About 99% of all houses in Broome have a sheet metal roof, known by its tradename of Colorbond. To make the sheets hang together and not fall off the roof, you need someone who can get up on top in 40-50°C heat and tek-screw the things down. That work and any guttering you may decide on if you were one of those posh pricks that didn't want the torrential rains in the wet season to run off in a spectacular, roof-borne fountain effect and into the surrounding pindan dirt, was the domain of the roof plumbers. Busy men, fucked in the head for working in those conditions, but worth a quid or two for the amount they could charge. Ours, it turned out, wanted to earn a bit more on the side.

However, Dodger had a rocky start with the Roof Plumber.

The bloke was extremely happy to have found a supplier of gear and would progressively grow to take on between six to eight ounces a week, but there were problems early on when he failed to take Dodger seriously.

Unknown to me, on about the third sale, Dodger had broken the golden rule and given him credit for a few hours. His explanation to me later was that the Plumber had been paying upfront without any hiccups, but on this occasion had convinced Dodger that he was collecting some dough later in the day and if he could have the ounces, he'd drop the cash off in the afternoon. Dodger was comfortable with the bloke and fell for it. Prick never turned up and it took us three days to find him.

We knew the job he was working and went there on the Monday morning, spotting him walking on top of the Colorbond roof.

Dodger told me to stay with the car, "It's my problem, I'll sort it," he said.

I rested my backside against the bonnet, folded my arms and watched how business was done, Dodger style.

Dodger gave him a friendly wave, climbed up onto the half-height scaffold and gestured for the Roof Plumber to give him a hand up. As they clasped hands, Dodger grabbed hold of him and dragged him off the roof. He clipped the handrail of the scaffold on the way down and landed flat on his back on the pindan and building rubble. There was an audible exit of air leaving his lungs and by the contortions of his face and the strange way his legs were rising up and down like a soon-to-be-dead fly, I figured he was in quite a degree of pain.

I was in two minds as to whether I should intervene, given that I wasn't keen on Dodger killing this bloke in front of me, but quite keen on retrieving our money. Sense won out. I stepped forward.

Dodger climbed down off the scaffold, cool as a cucumber and knelt in front of the guy's head. The Plumber couldn't talk, he was rooted, gasping for air and making small squeaky noises, like a punctured rubber duck.

"We had a deal that you would be finding me on Friday and dropping seven grand in my lap. Today is Monday and I'm still seven K shy."

The Plumber slowly raised his arm and pointed to his work ute, "Ubb ox."

"What?"

He sucked in some more air, "Glove box."

Dodger went to the ute, sat in the passenger seat and opened the glove box. Sure enough there was a plastic zip-top sandwich bag in there with seven grand inside. Dodger took his time, counting it out on the front seat before pocketing the cash.

With every second word interrupted by attempts to breathe, the Plumber stammered through a sentence that my brain eventually stitched back together as, "You've broken my ribs ya cunt, you didn't have to do that, I was going to pay you."

"Monday is not Friday, mate, either play by my rules or don't play. See ya when I need ya." Dodger motioned with his head to me, "We're out of here."

As we drove off, I could see the plumber still rolling around the dirt. He didn't appear at all well.

The following Friday he drove into our yard. I walked over to find out what he wanted, but I reckon I had it figured right. I had no need to be aggressive. "What's doing?"

"I haven't worked all week. I've got four broken ribs."

"And you want me to do what?"

"I need more whippa, how can we sort it out?"

"It's an easy fix mate. Dodger and I will be having beers here at one o'clock today. Bring a carton back with you, tell him you're sorry for fucking him around and you won't let it happen again."

He gave me a quick nod and drove out of the yard.

I could have set my watch by him. He pulled back into the driveway as the 1 pm news came on the radio.

A few months passed, Dodger and the Plumber had kissed and made up and he continued to pay up front without being asked.

And his ribs healed well.

He had been doing a lot of work in Derby, a town about 200kms north east, of Broome, so we figured most of the gear was going there, which made no difference whatsoever to us.

One day he dropped the acid on Dodger that there was a serious shortage of 'Green' around and asked if we had access to any?

As a matter of fact, we did. Pablo had plenty and had often asked me if I wanted to branch out and move some marijuana, but I had no interest in it and it would be hard to store due to the odour. I could think of ten reasons why we didn't need to venture into that commodity which included that we were doing quite well doing what we were doing anyway. We didn't really need the headache attached to dealing in it.

But I got outvoted, which was a bit weird as there was only me and Dodger who had voting rights, but sometimes I gave my mate the win, just to make him feel good; like he was part of the team.

When the next second-hand fridge arrived in Broome it had ten pounds of hi-quality marijuana sealed up inside. Then the next one and the next and so on.

The Roof Plumber took half of what we could get our hands on while Bill and Ben were usually good for the other half. The job couldn't have been any easier.

We had a serious problem storing the stuff if we had to hold it for any length of time though. We didn't have anywhere off site that was secure.

If we left it in the sealed fridges, you couldn't smell it but as soon as we unwrapped it, it stunk. Half of Broome would have recognised it from a kilometre away. It also took up a lot more space than the equivalent weight in 'White'.

Having it in the factory wasn't an option so Dodger did a deal with the Plumber.

He came in as an equal partner on the sale of the Gunja only, on the condition that he store it, he sell it and he was responsible for the cash coming back in.

It was difficult to know exactly how much cash was being generated because we had no idea what quantities he was selling it in, but fair to assume that with five pounds a time going out, it had to be large. If he was selling it off in $25 bags, then he would have been making an absolute fortune but to do that he'd need two hundred bottom feeders to supply who would have kept him busy all day. That didn't seem logical as he was holding down a decent job working flat out as a contracting roof plumber. There wouldn't have been enough hours in the day.

We calculated what a pound would be worth and agreed that was the base figure. To his credit, he came back to us many times, throwing more on the table than we had expected, so we came to trust him. Implicitly. Stupidly.

The Plumber's best mate was a South African bloke who had a bad limp. The story went that he had fought in the Rhodesian War under the prime ministership of Ian Smith. He'd suffered a severe gunshot wound in one leg which was now considerably shorter than the other. When he walked his head bobbed from side to side, so around town he was known as 'Sniper's Nightmare'.

"He's good for an arm or two a week," offered up the Plumber.

"What the fuck is an arm?" I asked.

"South African slang for half a pound. Over there they roll it up like a big sausage roll and it looks like a forearm."

"What's he do with half a pound a week?"

"Who fucking cares? Does it matter?"

"No, not really," I agreed.

"If you must know… do you know one-eyed Freddy?"

"Yeah, everyone knows him. You don't live in Broome and not know a six-foot seven indigenous bloke with a glass eye. Why?" I asked, wondering where this was going.

"He lives out in one of those places up the Broome Road out towards Roebuck."

"Yeah? So?"

"Sniper's a mate of his. He's entrenched into what he calls the township up there."

"Does he know we don't call them townships?"

"He's South African, who the fuck's gonna dissuade him?"

"Fair enough."

In July '93 the Plumber walked into the office and threw a small brick of compressed Hashish on the table. It was wrapped in cellophane with Chinese writing on it. Opened at one end, it was only part of what would have been a full brick at some stage. Top-end imported weed was going to be worth a hell of a lot more than the home-grown shit we were flogging off.

"We might have some opposition," he said.

"Wow! Check that out. Where did you get that from?" Dodger asked, showing a very healthy interest in it.

"Sniper's picked it up. I just met with him in town. He said someone is running around Broome trying to unload a heap of it. I borrowed it off him for thirty minutes to show you what's going on.

Don't tax it, he knows exactly how much is there, he weighed it in front of me."

"Who's selling it?" Dodger asked.

"He didn't offer up much on who the bloke is but happy to hand-ball him to us if we're interested."

I found this news interesting for a few reasons. Someone had to be well connected to get this sort of gear into the country. Had it come through Broome or Fremantle or one of a hundred other entry points? God alone knew, but the fact that it was imported meant an entirely different level of sophisticated drug dealing.

I had a quick moment of realisation that despite all we were doing, Dodger and I were only piss-ant amateurs, dipping our toes into a very professional area of commodity trading. While we considered a good week might have been able to buy us a ute, others in the same line of business were buying off freight ships and making enough money to float yachts in the marinas of Perth.

Dumb and Dumber

In August of '93, a couple of rough looking diamonds turned up in the yard one day, looking for work. They were driving a Ford station wagon and towing a very expensive speedboat. The car had Queensland plates on it and the boat trailer had a South Australian one on it. They claimed to have driven from Cairns across the top end and were looking for work and a place to stay.

It just so happened we were flat out with our legitimate building work and could do with an extra pair of hands out on site and around the factory, so I put them both on, starting the next day. I directed them to the caravan park on Port Drive where they could pitch a tent. Their accommodation wasn't my problem. As long as they turned up at 6:00 the next morning with safety boots and a good work ethic, we'd get on fine.

They asked if there was any chance they could leave the boat in the yard, it would make it easier for them to get around town till they got settled. I gave them the nod to park it up behind the shed where it couldn't be seen from the main road. I was happy to keep it in the yard, but I wouldn't be responsible for its security.

I'm not a boat person but I enjoyed water skiing and asked them when we were taking it out for a run.

"We'll let you know," was the less than enthusiastic reply.

Their names were Daniel and Derry. I'd nicknamed them Dumb and Dumber but that might have been a bit harsh because they turned out to be decent workers. They were on time every day and could read a tape measure. You couldn't ask for more than that.

The speedboat intrigued me. I knew fuck-all about the subject, but this thing looked terrific. A polished timber hull with about twenty coats of high-grade marine varnish on it. A full black canvas canopy over the top that must have been made specifically as it was shaped to blend and hug around the deck fittings and the steering wheel. The whole unit had to have been worth forty to fifty grand and these two were living in a tent. Something didn't quite add up. I noted that the dual axle, hot dipped galvanised trailer's number plate was held on by electrical ties which annoyed me a bit. Kind of like a Rolls Royce having its wing mirror held on with gaffer tape.

I pulled the cover off the boat one day to have a sticky beak. It was all class, the seats were genuine leather, chrome and brass fittings, more gauges on the dashboard than my car had. A beautiful looking piece of machinery.

I flicked the motor hatch latches and it opened automatically with a soft hiss of compressed air. The lubricated struts, like on the rear door of a station wagon, glided upwards, gently yet powerfully raising the large cover. The smell of clean oil and a faint trace of petrol met my nostrils, but it was my eyes that widened at the sight. A massive V8 engine, like some monster racing car filled the space, but half of it was missing. The motor must have been cooked and the heads had been removed.

I couldn't see any of the missing parts laying around, just the exposed piston heads staring back up at me. It was going to cost a fortune to get the motor back up and running again and, in Broome, you could double any capital city estimate.

I told Dodger about my little discovery and asked our other guys in the workshop to sound out Dumb and Dumber. There had to be a good story behind it.

A few days later we were briefed that D&D were more than happy to share their story. They had seen the boat parked up in someone's driveway in Cairns and decided that they could do with it. They backed their car up in the middle of the night, hooked it up and drove off out of town with it flapping out the back. At the first roadhouse they stopped at, they pinched a plate off a parked caravan and put it on the boat trailer. It wasn't till they arrived in Darwin a week later that they opened the canopy and realised they had pinched a dud. Not to be out done by this little set back, they decided to bring it onto Broome where they would try and flog it off.

They worked with us for about four months, I never had a problem with them and they kept turning up to work on time.

One day we were at the smoko table and Dumber was having a big whinge that he'd crushed a finger. The blood was accumulating under the nail and it was causing him a lot of pain. Not an uncommon injury in the building trade. I picked a match up off the table and explained to him and everyone else sitting there, how to fix the injury in thirty seconds.

"Go into the shed and over on the bench is a set of drill bits, get the smallest one you can find." I held up the match to demonstrate. "Rest it on the fingernail and spin the drill bit backwards and forwards using your thumb and forefinger so that it gently drills through the nail. When you hit the blood, the pressure will release immediately and the pain will disappear. You won't feel a thing."

The dickhead disappeared into the shed.

Two minutes later there was a hell of a commotion and he came back out the door a hundred miles an hour, screaming his guts out and abusing the shit out of me.

He'd found a one-millimetre drill bit but decided that using the mechanical drill press, instead of his fingers, was a better idea. Content with his theory, he turned the drill on and lowered it over his fingernail. The drill bit was brand new, ultra-sharp and as soon as it hit the nail it caught, dug in and passed through the nail and the finger, snapping the bit off in the process.

Dingbat now had a twenty-millimetre drill bit hanging out either side of his finger, blood pissing everywhere and it was all my fault.

I offered to pull it out using a pair of pliers, but he failed to see the humour in that.

I told Dumb to run him up to the hospital and not to bother sending us the bill, we didn't have workers compensation for idiots.

The boat disappeared.

To this day I have no idea whether someone with mechanical expertise bought it off them for a carton of beer or they drove it out to Willie Creek and burnt it.

The coppers turned up at the factory one day, which lifted the heart rate a bit, but they didn't want to speak to me, they were looking for Dumb and Dumber.

The pair of clowns had borrowed, or stolen, and that was the sticking point, a 4WD off someone they knew and had taken it down onto Cable Beach during the low tide to hoon around a bit. At some point they decided to walk up the beach and have a couple of beers at the resort.

About ten beers later they walked back down to drive the car out but in the meantime the king tide had come back in and the vehicle was rolling around the surf. The owner was telling the cops that it was stolen so he could claim insurance on it, D&D didn't need a stolen vehicle charge hanging over their heads and hung onto the story that the owner had given them the keys.

To be fair, they hadn't been the first to be caught out by the Broome tides. If you had owned a scrap metal yard in the town, you would have made a killing pulling submerged cars off the beach between Gantheaume Point and Willie Creek. It would have been good for four to five cars a week caused by people not being able to read a tide chart.

As well as being incompetent car thieves, they also tried to kill our boilermaker.

They had a battery problem with their car and hadn't been able to steal one from anywhere else. So, they decided to use a battery charger that was in our workshop to restore a bit of life back into the one they had.

Unknown to any of us working in the factory that day, they removed the screw-top caps off the battery, topped it up with tap water and hooked it up to the charger. The acid started to bubble away, as it should and they slid it under the steel work bench, out of sight. No problem with any of that, except the pair then decided to forget to tell anyone what they'd done, jumped in the dual cab with Dodger and drove off to a site job.

A charging battery should be in open space with decent air flow to take the fumes away and it certainly cannot have welding sparks anywhere near it.

Our boilermaker, Chris came along a couple of hours later and started to weld something up on his work bench.

Me and one of my casual labourers were in the office when 15 Kgs of battery exploded like fucking Krakatoa and we both shit ourselves. It felt like the roof had lifted off the building. The only thing that saved Chris from injury, was that the bolted down work bench sheltered him from the blast. The percussion left his ears ringing for a week.

When Dumb and Dumber came back later in the day, Chris met them in the yard and chased them around for ten minutes wanting to tear their heads off.

The next day they turned up with a brand-new battery under the bonnet and a carton of beer for Chris.

Early in December, Dumb stopped coming into work, he just didn't show up. Three or four days later I was sitting around the smoko table with the guys and asked Dumber, "Where's Daniel, is he coming back to work?"

"I don't think so," he replied.

"Where is he?"

"He's about seven K's out of town. But if you want to see him, you'll need to take a shovel."

"Funny, very fucking funny. Where is he?"

Dumber gave a shrug and headed back inside. It was what it was. D&D could have stood for drifters and deros. We had them all in Broome. By the time Christmas came round, Dumber had disappeared too.

A year later a Hollywood movie was released called *Dumb and Dumber*. I should have copyrighted my phrase.

Good Luck or Good Judgement

Broome has two very distinct weather patterns.

It's either dry and hot or it's full-on tropical rain with accompanying high humidity and heat that would kill any normal person. This wet season has the added inconvenience of the odd cyclone cruising past between December and March.

One such day in December '93 almost cost us thirty-five grand when Tropical Cyclone *Naomi* floated close to town.

When we originally took out the lease on our factory, the previous occupant had left a fairly new 6mm thick 2.4m x 6.0m sheet of mild steel checker plate in the middle of the factory floor. Being in the trade we knew it was probably worth a couple of grand. I asked the owner of the building what he wanted done with it and he told me that he had no use for it; the owner of it wouldn't be coming back and Dodger and I could have it. There was a fair chance that sooner or later we would find a use for it or flog it off ourselves, so we were happy to claim it.

We were shuffling benches and welders around the place one day and decided to move it over a bit, using the forklift blades to give it a nudge. Underneath the sheet, someone had cut a very neat hole in the concrete, slightly bigger than a shoe box and twice as deep. There was another steel plate covering the opening and recessed into the concrete lip. It was a professional job and at first appearance appeared to be an electrical pit of some description but there were no wires or junction boxes in there. Clearly it had been used as a safe in addition to the one that was in the floor of the office.

Occasionally we would use the 'pit' if we needed to store the dope, but it meant planning in advance. Obviously, no one else could be hanging around while one of us drove the forklift and the other stood guard in case someone rolled up to the locked front gate. It was only a five-minute job to expose the pit then push the checker plate back over, millimetre perfect to its original position.

We had put thirty-two ounces of newly arrived powder in the pit safe in a hurry because we still had some stock stored off site and didn't expect to be needing more for a week. We were also flat out with our real job and just needed some confidence that it was secure.

Wholesale value was just on thirty-five grand, but by the time Dodger sold it in a week or two it would have returned somewhere between seventy to eighty large. A lot of dough to be sitting in a concrete hole.

A cyclone had formed off the Gulf of Carpentaria and was travelling slowly towards the Kimberley, but we'd heard that shit before. We had a habit of punching in some numbers into the fax machine a couple of times a day and a return fax would print out the cyclone's position and any perceived threat. There was a five-dollar charge for the service every time you used it, but it gave us some confidence to go about our daily business with time to clean up or lock down if we needed too.

Dodger took a couple of blokes down to a cattle station halfway between Broome and Port Hedland to finish off some structural steel on a shed we had made and intended to be away for most of the week.

The cyclone gathered strength and the warnings started coming in that it was tracking towards Broome.

I woke up around 4:00 am to torrential rain and howling wind. At 5:00 am, Dodger rang me on the stations satellite phone to tell me they wouldn't be getting out anytime soon due to the flooding. Everyone on the station was camped up in the homestead for protection.

"The winds howling here, what's it like down there?" I asked him.

"The cat just flew past the lounge window… that give you a hint?"

"You keeping an eye on the water level?" He asked. A subtle hint to the pit safe keeping dry.

"Fuck me, I'd forgotten about that. I'm going now, speak to you later."

I was in a panic driving into the factory, water up to the bottom of the car door in places and palm trees and shit flying everywhere. When I pulled into the yard the front gate was open and Chris the boilermaker's car was parked up. I sprinted through the six-inch deep pindan slush and in through the PA door. The water level was just touching the steel plate in the middle of the workshop.

Fuck, fuck, fuck!

"Chris, what are you doing here?"

"Couldn't sleep, came in to check on everything here."

"Mate, I'm really grateful but you need to go home, like right now."

"It's okay, Kat, I'm happy to be here."

I had to get him out of there so I could salvage the dope if it wasn't already underwater.

"Chris, I'm serious, I need you to go home now. Please!"

"You sure?" He was pleading with me, trying to do the right thing.

"Go home mate, now. Can you lock the front gate on the way out without getting drowned please?"

I didn't have time to watch him lock the gate, as soon as I saw his car move, I locked the PA door from the inside, fired up the forklift and pushed the plate back.

Dry.

Thank Christ for that. The two shopping bags were damp with condensation on the outside, but the contents were as dry as a bone.

A couple of days later I took another look to see what had happened and the pit was full of red water and mud.

***

We had pulled a job in Halls Creek that involved some structural steel work, a few steel wall frames and roof trusses. We estimated that the job would take a week using four good blokes and were playing with the idea of transporting the steel work the 700km on a trailer that we could legally tow behind one of our vehicles. Another option was to put it on a semi and pay someone to deliver it to site.

Our rationale was that if we took two vehicles with four blokes, towing trailers, we could have all our manpower, tools and steel work travel at the same time. It would be marginally cheaper but a hell of a lot more convenient than using a transport company to deliver the steel.

Minor problem was that we didn't own a decent trailer to do the job, so we had to factor in the hire or loan of one suitable to carry the three-ton load. Another concern was how to load it both securely and legally to ensure that it would survive bouncing along the rough as guts National Highway Number 1 running across the top end from Broome to the Northern Territory border.

An opposition builder we knew and got on well with, offered us use of a ripper dual axle trailer he owned for a couple of cartons of beer. We decided to test run it with a full load first, just in case.

Once loaded up and strapped down it looked an ugly load. Most of the steel work had to stand vertically because it would have been over width if laid flat. It appeared top heavy, so we decided to take it for a run 30km out and back to the Roebuck Plains Roadhouse. Then we'd make a call as to whether it would survive the 700km trip.

At the regular Friday morning meeting with Bill and Ben picking up sixteen ounces, they wanted to know how quick they could get their fanny scratchers on another half-pound. They told us they were working with a truck driver who was moving it into Darwin and the bloke was passing through later in the day.

Getting our hands on it wasn't a problem, we just needed time to get it from where it was stored. For security reasons, it was very rare that we would have had any at the factory and needed a bit of time and patience to retrieve it.

"Does the bloke drive into Broome?" we asked.

"No, he does the Perth – Darwin run We usually have a beer with him at Roebuck Roadhouse, so he doesn't need to bring the road train into Broome."

"We were going to be out there for a problem of our own about lunchtime, if you're cashed-up, we can meet you out there then."

"You won't be meeting our bloke," Ben said with a smile on his face and a hint that we would snooker his customer.

"Yeah, we know how it works. So, midday at the roadhouse, right?"

"We're on, see you there."

This wasn't a bad pay day for us, selling thirty-two ounces in one day to one customer would have brought a new car. Thirty grand profit before lunch wasn't a bad day at work.

We drove out of the yard, towing the trailer and a very heavy load, on time to meet our lunch schedule at Roebuck Roadhouse. It only took us ten minutes out on the open road to decide we were kidding ourselves thinking we would tow this load to Halls Creek without killing ourselves or someone else. The load was swaying all over the road, it was heavy, uneven and was dragging the arse of the ute all over the place. We backed the speed off to a safe 75KPH and cruised on up to Roebuck Plains.

The coppers had the "T" intersection closed off and were running licence and breath tests on every vehicle coming in from the three different directions.

"This will be interesting," Dodger said.

"As long as they don't put dogs over the car," I replied, knowing that half a pound of amphetamine was in the toolbox behind my driver's seat.

The coppers directed us into the line that went through the roadhouse carpark and we were pulled up just short of the main building. Bill and Ben were standing against the handrail with coffee cups in hand. When they spotted us, one of them shook his head in a very slow, deliberate 'no' motion.

"What's that supposed to mean?" I asked.

"No idea. Stay calm Kat."

I did as Dodger suggested and watched a copper come to my window.

"Where you headed today driver?" asked the cop in a friendly manner.

"Right here actually. Just test driving this load. Going to grab a coffee and head back into Broome."

"No problem," he replied. "Can I see your licence? Had anything to drink today?"

I pulled my licence out of my wallet and had a joke with him that it was a bit early for a drink, but he made me blow in the bag anyway.

"All good," he said, looking at the breath test. "Give me a minute to check the licence." He walked off with my licence in his hand and did a lap around the ute and trailer. I could see him writing the rego down.

As he came back past the passenger side, Dodger asked him, "Can I go and get some lunch."

"No problem, I just need the driver to stay with the vehicle."

Great, thanks Dodger.

The cop walked over to a pop-up tent where the licence checks were being radioed in.

Five minutes went by and I could see a bit of body language and hand waving taking place, pointing my way. Meanwhile Dodger was standing at the counter ordering our coffee with Bill and Ben either side of him, all reassuring each other to, 'Just stay cool'.

Three coppers came back to the car.

"Would you mind getting out of the car please, Sir?"

"Sure, what's the problem?"

"Do you own the trailer?"

"No, I don't. Why what's wrong with it?"

"The number plate was stolen off a 1970 Valiant in Kalgoorlie three years ago."

"You have to be fucking kidding me?"

"No, I'm very serious."

Win, lose or draw, I had to convince them I didn't own the fucking trailer and prayed that their concentration stayed with it and didn't progress to the dual cab ute and the toolbox behind the seat.

I gave them a statement offering up all the details on who owned it, that I'd borrowed it the day before and I seriously doubted that the God bothering builder that owned it would have known about this. All of which was true.

The Dodger nearly had a heart attack when the prick finally came over with my cold coffee and I explained to him what was going on.

The police told us to unhook the trailer, it couldn't leave the car park. They would interview the owner, but I would be fined as the onus was on me being that it was hooked up to my car and I was driving.

When I realised they weren't going to pull the dual cab apart I started to relax a bit.

Bill and Ben gave us a hand to unhitch the trailer and grabbed the toolbox in the process. They came past the factory two hours later and dropped off the dough they owed us. It cost us a few bucks to leave the trailer out there and transfer the load to a semi a couple of days later but that was minor aggravation compared to what could have unfolded.

I had a falling out with the trailer's owner. He'd bought the trailer off a rogue and never received the papers for it. He had genuinely forgotten all about it.

I had no problem believing the story, that was how Broome worked, but that he was pissed with me for leaving the trailer parked up at the roadhouse was a bit much. He even insisted that I was responsible for returning it to him.

My counter-argument was that he should have paid the $450 fine. He declined.

***

After the Roof Plumber had dropped the half brick of Hashish on our desk, he continued to push the point that we should be a bit more proactive and get involved. "Another product we can move," was his sales pitch.

Dodger and I weren't so sure. Yes, it would be him selling a fair whack of it and making a dollar or two in the process, but we'd be the ones financing the project, as was the deal with him and the home grown weed we were buying off Pablo. He wasn't sticking his hand in his pocket to share in the outlay.

So, we gave him a bit of encouragement to get off his arse and do the reconnaissance on who was selling it and maybe who was behind bringing the gear into town, (if it wasn't the same bloke), what quantity was on sale and how much. We were thinking that if we gave him a bit of rope, he'd either come back loaded with information or, if he was full of shit, the project would just disappear.

Nothing more was said for a week.

"Okay, were on. Sniper's Nightmare introduced me to the bloke and he's keen. He's staying at that back-packers' joint next door to the push bike shop and wants to know what we want. He claims to have access to plenty, still wrapped up, two grand a brick. Wants to see the colour of our money."

"And if you're the lead man on this, why didn't you grab a brick or two while you were there?" I asked.

He ignored the question.

"So, when's this going to happen?" Dodger added.

"Both of them will be there any time after five today."

"Quantity?" Dodger asked.

"I don't know."

"You're a bit casual spending our money mate." I said it hoping the tone of my voice would let him know I was getting a bit tired of it all. The Plumber was too blasé for me. "How much does he think we're walking in there with?"

"I suggested five bricks, $10k."

Dodger gave me a sideways look and jumped in. "I've got a better idea. You're going in there and you do the deal on one brick."

"But…" He tried to get a word in.

"But fucking nothing. You don't know this bloke from a bar of soap and you want us to drop $10k on the table. You go in there, drop $2k on the table and we see what we're dealing with."

"I don't have two grand on me."

"You for real?" I asked. "The amount of gear you're moving and you don't have a lazy two on you?"

"No, it's put away."

"You are seriously fucking testing me," Dodger said and stepped back.

"Okay. We'll lock up the factory at 5:30 pm and we'll all go in together. Dodge and I will park up while you do the hard yards dealing with your new friend. When you walk back out, I want to know a damn sight more than I do now. His real name, phone number, what car he's driving, who he's banging. Pay attention and concentrate on what you're doing and who the fuck you're dealing with. Understand?"

The Plumber nodded and fucked off.

Dodger agreed that we were probably being led down the garden path, but there was an off chance that although the Roof Plumber was a scatter brain sometimes, just maybe, this was the real deal. And we couldn't ignore the fact that he was dropping a lot of dough into our pockets each week.

Two grand on the table would be a good relationship starter for everyone.

We were running a bit late and it was closer to 6:15 pm when we swung into the street, me driving, Dodger in the jump seat and the Plumber in the back with our two grand in his pocket.

It was dipping into the purple-black of a Broome evening and the brightest thing should have been the soft glow of an unbroken street light, but the road outside the rendezvous was ablaze with flashing blue lights.

"Jesus Christ!" Dodger screamed. "Keep driving, keep driving."

We cruised past the unmarked 4WD's and police vans at 10kph like a couple of locals looking for a pub. Three or four cops were standing at the back of a wagon with a tall overweight bloke in hand-cuffs. Sniper's was a couple of metres away with the same jewellery around his wrists.

"That's him. That's him," yelled the Plumber in my ear.

"The bloke you're supposed to meet?"

"Yeah, that's him. They got him."

"Fuck me," I said. "Is it any wonder I drink?"

The Real Estate Agent

KGB worked as a sales representative for one of the real estate companies in town. Without trying to put too fine a point on the subject, the woman would have put the horn on a Jelly fish.

Stunningly attractive. Short black hair, piercing green eyes. Well-educated, well-spoken and well put together. Every dangly and pointy bit was in the right place, firm and perfectly formed. Her long, slender legs with the curved calves of a long-distance runner were complimented by the designer clothes and high heels she preferred and that she seemed to have an unlimited choice of. She had exquisite cheekbones, a straight yet pert nose and a set of pearly whites that when she flashed a smile could melt your heart. Or stir other places. Every time I met her, I had to force myself not to stare. She was my perfect woman, a love borne of lust. A fantasy. She was also married and by the age of her two kids, probably in her early thirties when I first saw her.

KGB was not only gorgeous, she was also blessed with having a bit between her ears and was a partner with her husband in their real estate business. The husband had no hesitation in wheeling her out when he needed a bit of leverage on a sale and being how busy the housing market was at the time, she would have been making a decent dollar.

Yet for all her looks and brains she was most well-known, if not infamous, for a speech she had given at a Broome infrastructure seminar one night. She had been conned by her husband into believing the function would be a mixed affair but when she arrived, she was the only female in attendance. It was plain from his words and actions that he wanted her to dominate the room, not for the greater good of feminine equality, but as if she was being pimped out to advantage her husband's sales leads.

When invited to speak she opened with, "Well isn't this a nice sausage fest." Then she went on to give all the blokes in the room a serve about why they hadn't invited their female secretaries, sales reps, wives, or partners. Were they unworthy of being there? Did they not have any females in their lives that could hold a conversation on the topic at hand? She finished with, "When you go home tonight, have a little think about the competent women you have in your life who would have benefited by being here and maybe even benefitted you by being by your side tonight. Not for their atheistic qualities, but for their worth as human beings and their abilities to help, or perhaps, outshine you."

The speech, recorded for posterity by the reporter from the Broome Observer, went down like a lead balloon with some of her peers and her husband, but gave her credibility with the Broome elite, especially the women. It put on notice that her femininity should be seen as a strength, not a weakness.

The Dodger and I had had several interactions with her due to our overlapping legitimate business opportunities. She had visited us on site a couple of times, her in high heels, us in our ringing wet T-shirts, short pants and steel-cap boots. We'd visited her office to meet with mutual clients and on a couple of occasions we would catch up with her at the business 'after-hour functions' where we had the possibility to pick up more contracts. I used to look forward to those monthly after-hour events not for the business opportunities, but for the chance of meeting and talking to her. Come the July '93 function I'd been gutted to realise she wasn't there. Instantly bored, I'd struck up a convo with a newly arrived journo and me, him and Dodger went back to our yard and got pissed.

The following Monday, as I was driving through China Town, I saw her walking up the street with the sun blazing through her sheer dress. I nearly ran up the arse of the car in front while trying to line the sunlight up with the thigh gap. Good job I was in the ute on my own.

Dodger was in love with the woman. He had the hots for her something chronic and once said to me, "I'd crawl over a kilometre of broken glass to lick the dick of the last bloke that fucked her," which in Broome meant the same as, "I rather like that lady and feel we might be able to strike up a good relationship, if she were willing." Or words to that effect. The laughable thing was that on the occasions he had tried to talk to her he hadn't progressed too far. Being so infatuated, anytime he was in the same space he dribbled out the side of his mouth like a 15-year-old schoolboy, incapable of putting a coherent sentence together.

I looked again at KGB. Fuck it. Dodger wasn't here and I was. I couldn't help myself. I pulled over and, using the excuse of having missed her at the after-hours, decided to have a chat.

Sometime later, work had slowed for a few days as we were between jobs waiting on steel and materials to arrive by semi from Perth, a common delay for anyone trying to run a business in Broome. The labourers were told to go fishing for the day while Dodger and I left a temp to answer the phone and 'help herself to the fridge' while Dodger and I headed off in different directions at lunchtime to do other stuff.

Mid-afternoon, Dodger pulled up at my place and parked on the gravel out the front. The property had no fence, so it wasn't uncommon to park against the front verandah.

I didn't hear him arrive.

Now, if he'd bothered to park behind my ute he might have noticed KGB's car in front of mine, down the side of the house, half camouflaged by the Bougainvillea.

But he didn't.

He walked straight in the front door and through the house. There was no problem with that, even if the door had been locked, he had a key in his pocket. Waltzing through the kitchen and out onto the sundeck/pergola he spotted me with nothing more than a pair of shorts and baseball cap on, beer in hand. A millisecond later he sighted KGB sitting on one seat with her feet up on another. A few too many buttons on her blouse were undone and the magnificent silk, split to the thigh skirt she had on had been delicately rolled up to catch the sun. A glass of Semillon Sauvignon Blanc with an ice block in it was at her fingertips.

"Hey KGB, how you getting on?" Dodger managed to say, his usual tongue-tie overcome.

"Hi Dodgy, I'm good. You?" she replied, using the form of his name she always called him.

Dodger stood stock still. His hands tightly balled at his side. The muscles in his jaw were working overtime and when he turned his head stiffly to look my way, there was a real fury behind his eyes. Their usual blue had taken on a blackness. I wasn't sure and I didn't want to find out, but I reckon he'd have killed me there and then with no more thought than to squashing a mozzie. Only his voice was muted. Monotone and almost bored, he told me that he was only swinging past to let me know the semi had turned up and he would catch me later for a beer if I was interested.

"Have one now," I said pointing over to the beer fridge and glancing at the cheese knife with its three-inch blade sitting on the table. It was easily within his reach and I wondered if he was contemplating plunging it into my neck.

"Nah, I'm good. I'll see ya later. KGB," he said and almost gave her a formal nod as he turned away.

I knew Dodger for many a thing, but declining a beer, fuck me that was bad. A massive red flag. He'd never refused a beer in his life.

He was letting himself out through the kitchen when I caught up to him. Pointing down at my groin I said, loud enough for him but not KGB to hear, "Be careful of the broken glass mate. Watch your knees on it." I finished with the universal symbol of an imaginary cock going in and out of a mouth.

He turned around with a smirk that I guessed was somewhere between considering the consequences of a guilty murder conviction and breaking down into a writhing, sobbing mess.

Silently he mouthed two words, "You cunt."

I tipped an imaginary hat at him and returned to KGB. The bang of my kitchen door told me that there might actually be broken glass when I came back in.

Walking through to her I noticed that a blouse button had been done up and the silk was now rolled back down closer to her knees.

"Will Dodgy create a problem?"

"No, no. He's rock solid. Besides, I've got more on him than he has on me."

I sat back down beside her and rested my hand on the immaculate, smooth silk, teasing it back up the thighs as a test to see how my luck was holding out.

I was thinking that it could have been worse. It could have been her husband. I decided not to share my thought. Instead, I took her by the hand and led her through to the bedroom.

Dodger displayed a genuine strength of character in the days that followed. Holding his shoulders back and his head high with the surety that his moral compass would be the envy of lesser men. About a week later he started talking to me again. Never once, not ever, did he raise the subject of KGB in my company.

My relationship with KGB started off reserved and somewhat tame. In my mind I was batting out of my league and was apprehensive to rush in and play up like a performing seal, so the first couple of rendezvous were timid.

When I had first pulled her up in the main street, her piercing eyes and demeanour was that she wasn't unhappy to hang around and chat. At the time I wondered if I was reading more into the 'conversation warmth' than I was entitled to, but I rode the wave in hope.

Somehow our idle chat touched on property rents. I lied through my teeth that the place I was in was coming up for renewal and I was unsure if the rent matched the property. She jumped in quick, offering to swing past and give me an opinion. Weeks later she would tell me that her side of the conversation was as full of shit as mine.

I'd nearly broken my neck to get home in time to shower and shave.

About halfway through the coffee the touchy feely stuff started and while the coffee went cold the Gucci and Frucci hit the floor. The rest was history.

My second hard-on that first afternoon was when she asked me if we could see each other again.

As we got to know each other and loosen up a bit, I learnt that underneath the up-market, straight-laced Louis Vuitton outfits she was a no-holds barred, free-spirited, drop-dead gorgeous, prime of her life, female fucking machine. She was seeking pleasure and had no inhibitions whatsoever in how to go about achieving that. There wasn't a wrinkle, crevice or orifice that was out of bounds.

A couple of times she had turned up at my place having been to the gym first. Dressed in Lycra she was an absolute traffic stopper and sent my testosterone level through the roof. The three-quarter length, sprayed on gym pants with the, high, firm rear and her impeccable front-end looking like a Volkswagen boot lid, wound me up like a clock. It took about forty-five seconds from the time the flywire door was snipped shut till the Lycra hit the floor.

Only once did we arrange to meet up at the gym at the same time, being that we were both members there, but it was a complete waste of time. We spent ten minutes ogling and making stupid faces at each other from across the building before calling it quits and heading off to my place.

Approaching Christmas of '93, we managed a couple of dirty weekends away in Perth. She had legitimate business seminars and meetings to attend to and I had my own interests in steel suppliers, catching up with my kids and rendezvousing with Pablo.

KGB and I flew down and back up on different flights. She was red hot paranoid about being spotted by someone she knew so it helped ease some of her concerns. We stayed in a quality hotel in Hay Street and managed long and romantic dinners at expensive silver service restaurants. If there was a time and a place where the woman won me over it was when I held her hand and stared into her eyes on the balcony of that hotel during those warm summer nights.

While the meals and quality wine were magnificent, the after-dinner entertainment kept us awake half the night.

***

The week after Easter '94 I was in the beer garden of the Mangrove Hotel late on a Friday afternoon with Dodger and the Plumber. Dodger and I had been home to shower and put on some respectable clothes and had pre-arranged to meet up with the Plumber who had just driven in from Derby. He was to debrief us on his weekly sales and the cash reserves he had stashed under the front seat of his car.

It was rare that we would meet up like this. Normally he would swing past the factory or we would find him on the Saturday morning somewhere, but as a one-off this seemed like a good idea.

The Plumber's report was a standard procedure in that he'd sold so much white and so much green, that he was holding stock of this or that, or on a good week had sold out. The cash on hand came to such and such an amount and it was in his car or in the bag between his feet.

I spotted KGB and her husband walk onto the grass area and there was a slight hint that they had both spotted the three of us sitting at a table. A short discussion took place between her and her shadow, she walked off towards the bar and he made a beeline for our table.

Dodger and I knew the bloke well enough to say hello to but hadn't had a great deal of interaction with him. Neither of us assumed he would have known the Plumber.

Given I was banging his wife at least twice a week I was getting ready for a full-on scrap in the beer garden. Dodger saw him coming too and said, "What's he want?"

"Fuck knows," I said and started to get up.

He approached nice as pie and said, "Hey Kat, Dodger, how you guys going?"

"All good and you?" I answered, forcing myself to sit back down and chill the fuck out. This might not be going where I thought it was.

"Not bad, thanks. Mind if I grab the Plumber's ear for a minute?"

"Of course, no problem."

With that, the Plumber stood up and they walked about twenty metres or so away for a chat.

"What the fuck do you think that's about? They know each other?" asked Dodger.

"No fucking idea, I thought he was going to take me on over his missus."

"So did I. And I'd have held you down while he kicked the fuck out of you," Dodger said and gave me a wide grin.

"Thanks, mate."

"Anytime."

"Your fucking knees stopped bleeding?" I asked.

"Cunt."

Laughing, I glanced over Dodger's head and gazed at KGB. From this distance it was hard to see her eyes, but she wasn't giving me much back. If anything, she looked a little confused.

The Plumber came back to our table and the husband kept walking with a, "Thanks boys, keep well."

KGB, with two drinks in hand, joined her old man at a table set up for a dozen patrons. I recognised a couple of them as the top end of town hierarchy.

"I'm really looking forward to hearing about your relationship with him," I asked the Plumber.

"Fuck-all. He just wants another ounce of Gunja over the weekend."

The Dodger and I nearly fainted.

"Are you fucking serious? How long has this been going on? How long you been selling to him?" Dodger asked.

"Since about ten minutes after you brought the first load in. Why, what's the problem?"

"No problem at all. I'm just in shock that our gear is being sold that high up the Broome chain of command. His wife gets into it?" I asked, curious as hell to know if KGB was a pot smoker.

"Don't know, I've never spoken to her. Anyway, don't be so fucking naive Kat. You don't reckon those fuckers get on it? They're all on it. Just because you're a cleanskin doesn't mean the rest of the world is. You think if they wear a tie occasionally they must be straight? See the bloke he's sitting next too, the bloke with the blue shirt on?"

"Yeah, I know him, he's a big noise in the Chamber of Commerce."

"Correct. Well, he's good for an ounce a week on most weeks. He'd be sharing it with everyone else at that table."

"Probably not everyone at the table," I said. "The bloke on the very end is a detective. I use to live next door to him. Andrew's his name." Turning to Dodger I asked, "You know this was going on?"

"Nup. News to me."

"Un-fucking believable."

I pushed the Plumber a bit more, trying to get my head around who's who in the Broome hierarchy zoo and what their drug of choice might be. "Any of them buy Whippa off you?"

"Not that mob. No. The subject hasn't come up. That doesn't mean none of them are getting on it, it just means I'm not selling it to them. For all you know, one or two of them might be buying it off one of your other dealers. Don't for one minute discard the idea."

"Yeah okay, I get the drift. You just be careful who you're selling to and do not ever mention Dodger and my name. We on the same page here?"

"Of course. Goes without saying."

I saw KGB get up and head off for another bar run so I grabbed our empty pot glasses and stood up.

Dodger grabbed me by the shirt, he knew what my game plan was. "Easy Tiger."

"Yeah, I'm cool mate."

The Plumber had no idea what we were talking about.

I slipped in beside her at the bar.

"You're looking as stunning as usual."

"Thank you, Mr Smooth. I think that's the first line you used on me, Kat."

"It worked, didn't it?"

"Still does, thanks for noticing."

Pointing to the table she had her back to, I said, "I didn't know you sat on the Board of the Broome Mafia."

"Very funny. It's just another sausage fest, would-be's, could-be's and wannabes. Their bullshit conversation is doing my head in. Can I join your table?" she asked, teasing me.

"Come on over, you can sit on my knee. I dare you. Let's see how quick their meeting shuts down then," I joked.

"I have a better idea, you home at 6:30 in the morning?"

"For you I will be. Door will be unlocked."

"See you then, *Mon Chat*."

***

In May '94, the relationship had been running at full gas for around ten months when one afternoon she got a bit teary eyed with me and pulled up the courage to tell me we had to give the game away. It was very thoughtful of her to have held this revelation until after we'd spent the previous hour trying to dislocate each other's hips.

Her conscience was wearing her down, two kids, husband, three or four property assets and business interests. She was sure that doing pelvic exercises with me would become common knowledge and she just didn't want to go down that road.

Now, I'm not a callous prick. I really was hurt that she was giving me the flick.

I'm sure there would be millions of examples where a relationship starts off based on lust and the unspoken rule is that it starts and finishes right there and no one else on earth need know or be hurt.

That's how we got off the ground.

But people grow on each other, they enjoy being in each other's company, maybe even with clothes on. Making idle chat, looking into each other's eyes, digging deeper into their character, their interests in life and their background.

The chemistry slowly changes and a spoonful or two of 'love' gets blended into the equation. I was guilty of that. Ah that's bullshit. It was much worse than one or two spoonfuls and I knew it. It was a long time since I'd felt like this. My guts ached like they were full of lead. I lay awake till the small hours. I was almost fucking crying watching fucking *Neighbours* for Chris'sake. Although that might have been more to do with the actors on Ramsay Street than my feelings for KGB, but the upshot was I had loved her. Was loving her. Fuck it.

As much as it pained me, I had to admit she was right on all counts.

My selfish self-assessment was that I had never harboured any thoughts of being a stepfather to her kids or considered the consequences of splitting up her family bubble. The one subject that had never come up between us was, "what happens next" and that probably reflects badly on me because I'd never stopped to consider it. At least she had thought it through. I'd never considered any extension of our relationship past its present commitment. But that didn't change the fact. I loved the woman.

Nothing would have pleased me more than to have taken her out for dinner or a long lunch somewhere in Broome, looking out over the bay or the Indian Ocean, holding hands over a white tablecloth, a slab of grilled Threadfin Salmon and a respectable bottle of plonk on the table. But I was dreaming. It was never going to happen without some life-changing decisions being made by both of us.

If we had walked hand in hand into any restaurant in Broome, her husband, who was just as well-known and respected, would have been walking in the front door before the main meals arrived.

In fairness to her, she had a lot to lose, whereas I had nothing. I was freelancing, answerable to no one. The only person that might have wanted to know where I was or what I was doing was Dodger and I wasn't married to him. Nor of course, could I talk to him about her.

Also, being such a highly respected member of the community, if it went pear-shaped for her the shit would stick.

To ease the pain of the breakup I tried to tell myself that I was time poor and running a legitimate, respectable business whilst also keeping half of Broome fuelled up to the eyeballs with speed and weed. I couldn't have taken on a bigger commitment with her.

Truth was, she could have hung around forever; I would have found time.

Alone and desperate not to be a sad fuck, I threw myself and Dodger into making more money.

But that had its own problems.

The Problem with Cash

More dope, more money. Nice problem to have, you'd think. For me, it simply meant trying to find more places to hide it in.

In the early days, we were pulling maybe a grand or two a week in each, twice the average wage of a good paying job. Doesn't sound like a lot but it accumulates quickly when you have nothing to spend it on. A few beers and groceries each week didn't make a dent in it. By the end of the second month we would be five big ones a week in pocket. At six months it was ticking over at around twenty grand a week… profit… each.

Walking down to the local high-street bank and depositing that type of cash was a one-way ticket to jail as soon as the cops picked you up for unexplained earnings. I couldn't leave it in the work safe and in hindsight I was being a bit too laid-back about where I stashed it. By the time I took stock, I had a lot of places where there was dough hidden. That wasn't good for me or the security of my money.

I had started off having it in the house.

There was an exhaust fan in the bathroom that went out through the wall horizontally, not vertical into the ceiling. Only three screws to remove the face plate and wrapped up tight in plastic was maybe $30k. In a hollowed-out book in a half-baked bookshelf was a lazy $10k. In my ute I had a timber rack that supported thirty cassette tapes. It was a first-class job. I'd made it myself and it would have survived most scrutiny. Any fleabag breaking into the car would have gone straight for the tapes. Underneath it was a small trap door with a very small bolt lock. Impossible to see, you would need to run your hand underneath to know there was a void there. There would have been $15 - 20k in there. If you took the back off the washing machine, there was another twenty-five. Completely remove the bottom draw next to the sink that had my tea towels in it and there was a big payday there. And on it went. On a good month I'd have upwards of $250k knocking around. That's a quarter of a million fucking dollars. It was beginning to stress me.

I had a betting account with the Australian-wide TAB organisation that had forty large in it at one stage. That didn't last long though as the two regular blokes on the counter knew me and rolled their eyes when I'd put five grand into the account each week and then place a seven dollar, 'Favourite Numbers' bet. They had to be asking themselves, "What's this fucker up too?"

Plus I'd read that the TAB was coming under the same scrutiny as banks in regard to dodgy accounts, so I pulled the dough out.

Then I stumbled onto a brilliant solution. Well, I say I did. Rather, it walked through the front gate and presented itself to me.

Otto had been in Broome for a very long time and, with all due respect, he looked like he might have arrived with the founding party of Sir Frederick Broome himself. Weather worn and leathery, he had actually come out to Australia as a five-year-old when his parents legged it out of Germany after World War I. The only give away to his heritage was his name, he spoke and swore better Aussie than me.

He had owned a few industrial blocks of land in Broome for years, but life was tapering off for him. His wife was over the heat and had recently moved back to their second home in Dunsborough, an up-market, rich-retiree village on an idyllic piece of coastline in the far southwest, so Otto was slowly selling off his assets in town to transition his own life back below the 26th Parallel.

The last property he was hanging onto was a six thousand square meter, mostly vacant, block off Clementson Street. Its life had been a lay-down area for a variety of freight companies but the last mob that had leased the yard had gone bust and owed him money. Due to a lack of care, spinifex was breaking up through parts of the concrete and the shed that sat in the middle was beginning to look a bit sorry for itself. Even the security fencing was beginning to weep down towards the ground in places and that had allowed a few of the local kids to make their way in with spray cans and the odd bottle of grog.

Otto had lost interest in doing anything with the block other than sit on it; financially, not literally. He was sick of dealing with people and wasn't interested in the head fuck of leasing it out and getting burnt again. Obviously he wasn't short of a quid and there didn't appear to be any urgency to sell it.

The property had two rough-as-guts transportable modules, called port-a-cabins in the rest of the world, but only ever referred to as dongas in Oz. They sat, graffiti covered and smelling faintly of piss, in the northwest and northeast corners of the main shed. Neither of them would have been worth a cold pie. One had been used as an office and the other was used in recent times by Otto as somewhere to stay when he was in town sorting out his affairs. It wasn't five-star accommodation, you wouldn't have let your mother-in-law stay there.

Otto asked me if I would act as a caretaker for him so he could return down south, he didn't need to be hanging around Broome. The deal paid a hundred bucks a month to drive past occasionally, maybe let someone in from time to time to park up a vehicle and I could use it for my own business storage use if I wanted. Pretty sure Otto meant as a lay-down yard for my building materials, but he didn't have to know what I thought about his offer.

I had noted that the old accommodation donga was sitting on a galvanised steel chassis made up of 200mm x 100mm rectangular hollow section blanked off at each end to keep the critters out. On the other donga was a spare wheel that was attached to a swing bracket and welded on, like you see on the back of a caravan. The wheel had never been off the bracket in its life, it was flat and perished, of no value to anyone, especially after I put a knife through the side of it to prove the point.

It took me a couple of hours one Saturday afternoon to move the wheel and bracket over to the RHS chassis and re-weld it on one end. The result was that I now had a six meter long safe, half a meter off the ground, watertight, with the opening looking like a spare wheel rack that had been there for thirty years. No one was ever going to cut the lock off to pinch a wheel that was useless. If they had, the swing bracket would have opened ninety degrees and exposed the opening and a shit load of cash wrapped in plastic. Each bundle had 0.9mm Mig welding wire tied to it so if it needed to be pushed back, I could use the wire to pull it forward. It was never going to get lost. Shining a torch down the tube showed a line of interwoven bundles of grey $100 and yellow $50 bank notes.

My only other concern was fire, but I didn't lose too much sleep over that as the majority of the building was steel and clad in Colorbond. I disconnected the power to the donga from the main board out in the driveway and considered my dough was now safe in the one place.

The Dodger and I never shared hard facts on where we stashed our cash. It wasn't good business sense to know what the other partner was up too. If either of us got rolled or the dough got pinched and only one other person knew about it, well you can imagine the stress it would have put on our relationship.

I knew Dodger moved some of his earnings back to Perth though.

He had to fly back down south to sort out ongoing ex-wife issues at one point and I offered to take him to the airport. When I picked him up, he was dressed like a pox doctors' clerk, collared white shirt and tie, carrying a leather briefcase. I nearly wet myself when he walked out of the house.

"And who the fuck are you meant to be?"

"For your information, shit head, I am a respectable member of the Broome business community on a work-related trip to Perth. I would be grateful if you would refrain from using such uncouth language in my presence."

"And what's in the briefcase, your fucking comic books?"

"A hundred grand to be exact."

Despite Otto's yard coming to my aid, I still had too much cash. I remember thinking that very thought whilst standing on the high ground looking across Roebuck Bay. Two or three nights a month you can stand up there as the receding tide drifts out and the rising moon offers up the 'Staircase to the moon'. It is only the moon light shining across the wet sand, but it creates a natural phenomenon that gives the illusion of a staircase stretching from the bay to the moon.

Gazing out, I tried to think about where I could hide more dough. What I needed was a bent bank manager. How true it is. Visualise something fucking hard enough and it shall appear.

The Bank Manager

Melbourne 1970

Thomas Harold James Berryman, commonly called Tommy, joined the Greater Victorian Savings and Investment Bank, commonly called the Great Vicky, as a clerk at eighteen years of age in 1947.

He climbed steadily through the ranks, proving to be a conscientious, well-balanced (a handy trait in his choice of job) and meticulous member of the establishment.

At the relatively young (by bank standards) age of 40, he was promoted to manager of a quiet suburban branch in South Melbourne.

Tommy recognised the heavy-handed knock on his office door that came most Mondays around lunchtime. The rap-ta-tap-thud was always the same. As were the two thugs who walked in without waiting for permission. It shouldn't have happened like that of course. Usually, Tommy's office was locked from the inside. Only he and the deputy manager had a key and the latter only in case Tommy dropped dead during the working day. But every Monday at five minutes before noon, Tommy rose, inserted the key into the heavy oaken door and turned the lock, before retaking his seat behind his green-leather topped desk. His two visitors stood in front of his desk and glared down at him, making their best attempt at intimidatory stares. They worked for the General Secretary of the Federated Ship Painters and Dockers Union, a man called Alfred William McManus. Tommy and Alfred were cousins.

With no pleasantries being offered up, the two men opened a briefcase and pulled out a paper bag, sitting it in the middle of Tommy's desk.

Inside were 32 'Ghosts'. Bank passbooks, each made out in a different false name, each untraceable. Inside the cover of the passbooks would be a fawn paper pay slip with an amount of cash inside, representing the wages of the ghost, a fictitious person, employed through the Union and who had allegedly worked a shift or shifts at the Melbourne waterfront during the previous week.

In a separate envelope would be Tommy's weekly two percent commission for his role in overseeing the account deposits and occasionally, withdrawals. It would also be Tommy's responsibility to secure those passbooks until his cousin, Alfred, requested them on the following pay day.

'Ghosting' wasn't invented by the FSPD. The 5th Governor of New South Wales, Lachlan Macquarie was caught out in the early 1800's when he registered an assortment of Indian boys, aged between six and seven years-old, who he had 'purchased' as commissioned army officers. For not a short time he had collected their pay and had a jolly time spending it on their behalf no doubt. The Colonial Secretary back in London had been less amused. All the FSPD did was expand the concept and make it a lot more streamlined.

Tommy didn't touch the paper bag.

"Take a seat for a minute please, I need you to be witnesses."

The two round face goons, straining the seams of ill-fitting suits and sweating over too-tight collars that had badly tied Union ties hanging from them, one too long and the other too short, looked quizzically at each other. With a shrug, they plonked their fat arses down in the leather low-back chairs in front of Tommy's desk. This was the first time they had stayed in the office longer than thirty seconds.

"You will both be well aware that I have had a long-standing arrangement with your boss for some time now."

The boofheads nodded in agreement.

"And you know who your boss is, in relation to me?"

They shook their heads this time.

"Ah, you see. That's where you went wrong. He's my cousin."

The two men looked to visibly pale against the rich brown leather of their chairs.

"I need to ring him now and you will be witnesses. I'm going to tell him that a month ago my commission was forty dollars light. Three weeks ago, it was another forty under. Last week it was fifty. That is not the agreement we have in place.

"I'll tell him that you and I will count out what's in the bag here now and if it's short by one cent then all bets are off. I'll take what I'm owed out of one of the accounts and close them all this afternoon. He can go back to hiding the cash under his fucking pillow."

The two sitting opposite had recovered from their initial shock but now seemed to be going a cherry-red. Tommy wondered if their respective blood pressures had risen so much they might both have heart-attacks. That would be inconvenient.

"You can't do that," said short-tie.

Tommy took the bank-issued revolver he'd had sitting on his lap and placed it beside the telephone on his desk as a show of bluff. The two men, who were now candy-striping between flushed red and shocked white, gasped. Tommy stifled a laugh and kept a straight face.

Firearms were allocated to bank managers in the event of a hold-up and the rules were that it should remain in the manager's care whilst in the bank. After hours it was required to be locked away in the bank vault. Tommy, for reasons mostly to do with his errant cousin, carried it on his person all day, every day.

If you were connected to the FSPD it was seen as a bit of insurance for your own welfare, especially where money was involved.

"How much is today's drop short?" he asked.

Slowly and without being able to hold eye contact, long-tie admitted, "Fifty."

Tommy knew that the funds were being taxed somewhere between the FSPD Secretary's office and his own door, but couldn't be absolutely certain who was doing the taxing. He now knew that his assumption was correct and these two clowns would be shitting in their pants.

If the Secretary ever found out they had their hand in the till and had been stealing from a trusted ally the reputation of the FSPD would see them both fitted out with concrete boots and going for a swim in the middle of Port Phillip Bay.

"I'll tell you how this is going to work," Tommy explained.

"Next Friday there will be three hundred dollars extra, one eighty you dudded me on plus a penalty fee to compensate me because you took me to be an idiot."

"Bu—" short-tie started.

Tommy cut him off. "Or," placing his hand on the phone, "I ring my cousin."

***

Six months later, two days before Christmas 1970, three blokes dressed as Santa Claus burst into the suburban bank, waving handguns around and screaming in a bad parody of Hollywood, "This is a hold-up, no one move."

Tommy, instead of ensuring the door to his office was securely locked, rose to investigate the noise, ignoring all the bank security protocols. He unlocked the door and was met by a gunman and pushed back inside. As he stumbled back, the bandit pointed his gun at Tommy's head and screamed, "If you move, I'll shoot you."

The gun remained pointed at his head for the next seventy-five seconds till the call came, "We're hot, we're hot. Go, go, go." One of the bandits had a police radio scanner to his ear and had been listening in on their chatter.

Tommy was rattled badly by the hold-up and would suffer anxiety for years. He wasn't too concerned about the fifteen grand that was stolen that day, it wasn't his money to lose sleep over, but he had day sweats every time he recalled the bandit walking into his office and imagining what would have happened had he, Tommy, still been sitting in his chair with his hand on the bank-issued revolver.

How would that have unfolded?

He never really believed he would ever be in a position, or have the nerve, to shoot someone inside his bank. But would the bandit have fired?

What upset him most was that some prick had pointed a gun at his head from one foot away and had threatened to kill him.

He did not recognise the stature or the voices of the bank bandits that day and no one was ever charged over the hold-up.

In his own mind he believed the dots were connected straight back to the FSPD. He tendered his resignation at the bank in February 1971. He hadn't spoken to Alfred since the day of the robbery. Six months after Tommy left the bank, Alfred washed up dead on the banks of the Yarra.

***

Twenty-three years after his bank career came to an untimely end, Old Tom drove into our yard one morning asking for some advice on a welding repair job on the caravan towing hitch hanging off the back of his 4WD. It had a crack in it and the choices were either throw it in the bin, buy a new one or have it re-welded. It was a good call on his behalf not to ignore the problem, pulling a two-ton caravan with it wouldn't be a good idea. People get killed with those failures.

The quote he showed me on a brand new one was outright theft, indicating that there were far bigger crooks in town than Dodger and me.

I called over Chris, our boilermaker, for an opinion and he agreed it could be repaired. It would need to be ground out, welded properly and would take an hour.

The old fella looked like he could do with 'Mate's rates' and he reminded me of my dear dad, so I cut him a deal.

"Carton of Melbourne Bitter and you can have it about lunchtime."

"Deal, thanks."

On his return we refitted his newly painted, thoroughly repaired, looking like new, towing hitch. He was thrilled to the back teeth.

As it was a Friday we usually threw a carton or two on the outdoor shaded smoko table for the labourer's and anyone else hanging around and chuck a couple down. Old Tom's carton was good timing. I added one out of our fridge and we got into it.

I invited him to join us.

We had a bit of a chat and I learnt he was a retired Melbourne bank manager. He and his missus had been on the road for 18-months and arrived in Broome a few months earlier. He was fed up with driving and camping and had decided they would stay put for a while. Having rented a two storey quality town house in the street behind me, I figured he must have had a quid in his back pocket.

My impression was that he was a bloke who had been craving a bit of freedom and male company by the way he mingled, joked and swore his way around our piss-up table for the next couple of hours. Another carton came out and the five or six of us still there gave it a nudge. When time came to call it quits Tommy had his dancing shoes on and didn't want to leave. He'd had as much to drink as the rest of us, but I reckoned he was in no state to drive. Instead, I offered to lock his car up in the factory, drive him home and we'd sort it out in the morning.

He agreed.

Within a week, Tommy had a job working three half days with us doing our book work, answering the phone and sorting out some accountancy head fucks we had. Employing him was one of the best business decisions we would ever make.

Within two weeks you'd have thought he owned the place. He was there every day by his own desire and instantly became a father-figure, driving the business with experience and a professional touch. A real asset to Dodger, me and the business.

I met his wife and concluded that one of the reasons he hung out at the factory so much was that he was happier being in our company than hers. She was real hard work and I was a little surprised he hadn't 'lost' her in the desert when they'd been out there. I doubt she would have given him anymore than the time of day for the last twenty years.

By the end of the third week, Tommy took me to one side and discretely broached the subject of the illegitimate cash coming into the business and how it was allocated.

In simplistic form, Dodger and I had the same problem in that we both had ex-wives who were fucking gold diggers and their child maintenance payments were based on our annual income. That income was determined by the tax office. The more money you earned, the more you paid out. Even a fuckwit knew the answer to that one.

Dodger and I already had an advantage. Twenty percent of our business income was cash.

We had a lot of people walking in the front gate who wanted a few lengths of steel, cash. An off cut of checker plate, cash. A welding job, cash and so on.

It wasn't business rocket science. If some character wanted thirty sheets of pink 'Blush Cheeks' Colorbond, we'd order it in and he would pay cash. We'd pocket the cash and transfer the material costs onto a legitimate project, in theory adding expenditure to that job and reducing the profit. That job, being legitimate would be reported in our annual accounts. The only way that came unstuck was if the ATO sent an auditor to inspect the job and noticed the project was clad in 'Surf Mist' or 'Manor Red' and there was not a blushing cheek in sight.

The chances of that happening were zero.

Fact was, if we could hide most of the cash or shuffle it around somehow to record the smallest of profits on the books, then the business would be barely breaking even and the poor old tax office would have to cut us some slack.

Like I say, not rocket science, but even I was surprised at how quick Tommy picked up on it. Within a month, on paper, we had a business that was just surviving. In reality we were killing a pig.

Instead of looking at buying new equipment we were leasing it, or Tommy was sourcing second-hand machinery from bankruptcy auctions.

Materials were transferred and hidden in legit jobs. Some cash was used to pay untraceable debts like sub-contractors who were running the same scam. The place was humming and we still had a safe full of cash for Friday afternoon beers. Add in a couple of legitimate rorts like the tax zone rebate for living and working above the 26th parallel and Tommy claiming a heap of our bottle-shop purchases and counter lunches as 'Entertainment Expenses' and it all added up, or rather subtracted down to us not paying a lot of tax.

Our former bank manager was driving the business like it was BHP and the gold diggers would choke on their next assessment notice.

However, cash laying around the business continued to be a headache. It was compounded by the fact Dodger and I had twenty times that problem with cash from drug sales that Tommy was not doing the books for.

Over a beer one day he started regaling me with a few stories about the banking industry that had my ears prick up.

"You know, son," he said, taking a long pull on his can of VB. "The most infamous white-collar criminals in Australia are not the guys with the sawn-offs robbing the banks."

"No, Tommy?" I said, "Who are they then?"

"The fucking bank managers. People like what I used to be. We could rip off more fucking money from the system than all the shotguns on the continent."

I allowed my plastic chair, previously balancing up on its two shaky hind legs, to come back down onto all-fours. "I'm listening."

"In the 1960's through to late 1970's the greatest con was the 'Seven-year itch'."

"I thought that was a marriage issue."

"Not in banking terms.

"There was a government directive that any bank account not accessed for seven years would automatically have the funds redirected to, no surprise, the government coffers. Fucking thieves."

I nodded in sympathy and reached for another drink. Tommy ploughed on.

"But the shifty bank managers knew all about it and were the persons responsible for reporting the dead accounts. Ha, what a golden egg. All we had to do was be a bit sharp. If the Feds were going to sweep in and take the money after seven years, we would watch the accounts from five years onwards."

"Yeah, but I don't get it. How does a not-accessed account help you?"

"Well, you see… let's say Kat McKatkill has an account that hasn't been touched. Yes?"

"Yeah, the name sucks, but go on old man."

"As the seven-year date got closer, a good operator would take a drive and see what the last known address looked like, maybe speak to a neighbour, tell them some bullshit story to discover when they'd last seen poor old Kat. Had they any clue where he was? That sort of thing. The prize catch was someone who had died and had no known relatives, probably no will, hence, no one other than the original account holder, Kat in our case, would have known about the account's existence."

"Okay," I said, staying up with the gist of it. "Go on."

"The bank manager would be watching the account and at some stage would decide the funds would be better served elsewhere. The trick was for the manager to pull the signatory card from the branch files, reinstate it with another signature, probably from an accomplice and issue a new bank book with the blue-light dodgy signature on the back page. Either the manager or his accomplice would then hit every bank at their leisure and pull out all the funds. The signature on the withdrawal form would perfectly match the one in the back of the passbook and if push came to shove, it also matched the original that was held in the issuing bank branch's safe. There was no hurry, they took their time and never pulled out large amounts in one hit that might draw suspicion.

"Another seven years later, whoever the manager might be then, would report the account as being expired, with no funds recorded. A lot of good people made a lot of good money."

There was no doubt in my mind that Tommy was speaking with firsthand experience.

A few days later I'd let him use my car to go into town to do the banking. When he came back he waited till there was only me in the office. "You have rocks in your head, Kat."

"Pardon?"

He pulled out a wad of cash and threw it to me.

"And?" I asked.

"I dropped a pen on the floor of your ute, when I went looking for it, this fell in my hand."

"Thanks, I'd forgotten about that."

"You need to be more careful where cash is concerned, Kat. Why don't you put the cash from the work safe into the bank?"

"Time you retired Tom… it would show up as unexplained income, the ATO would be on to it, I'd be fucked. We can't pay it out to ourselves as profit as the gold diggers would get their fanny scratchers on it."

"Listen to me son," he said, taking a seat. "There are ways around these things."

"Go on."

"These days if you open a bank account you need to supply identification, Tax File Number, address, phone number, right?"

"Yep."

"Well, those records are photocopied, put in a file and held at the branch. There is no fucking big warehouse where every hardcopy of every document from every bank in Australia is kept. It is the branches responsibility. What the head office of each bank branch receives is a faxed, ticked check list that the documents have been sighted and signed off by a branch official. If it was, or had the potential to be, a large account then head office might request the originals but that is rare. Big businesses don't run their banking from suburban branches anyway.

"But consider this. What if the documentation didn't exist, what if the only card the branch had was a false signature card? With some intervention, the information supplied to open the account was all false and the file, numbered to the account, couldn't be found, lost, misplaced, didn't exist?"

He had my attention. "So, an account is open, usable, but has no traceability to it. Is that what you're saying?"

"That's exactly what I'm saying," he replied with a grin on his face.

"What about basic requirements like contact phone number and address?"

"All bullshit, they won't exist," he answered. "Banks don't ring customers to ask them how their day is going. In forty years, the only time I rang a customer was to return a call from them. Yes, you supply a number but invent one, it won't be valid. An address is a little problematic because they want to send you a statement now and again, but you can nominate now that one not be sent out. Your excuse is that you can check your account through the card they issue to you and you have no requirement for a hard copy being posted out. However, if you lose a card and you need another one you will need to go into the branch where the account is held, to avoid scrutiny from a different branch and tell them you will pick it up from the bank in a week or two when you're next in."

I was thinking on my feet as he talked. I had access to a Broome post office box that didn't belong to me. Old Otto, the owner of the block on Clementson Street, gave me the key to his as part of my 'caretaker' role when he left town. The only mail that had ever been in there was junk mail and a Broome Shire rate notice which I'd redirected. The key to it was in our safe, under Tommy's feet.

"I can probably sort a postal address," I said. "How much dough can you plonk into the account?"

"That is of very limited interest to the bank, they just want to know they have your business. If you have an account with them, their business model is that you are likely to approach them should you need a housing loan or credit card and that's where they make their big quid. They don't give a fuck where the decimal point on the account sits. With the exception that it is not millions, that would be a red flag. And you don't walk in there with a brown paper bag dripping cash. You'd deposit relatively small, non-uniform amounts, so they look like a business account, nothing over ten grand at a time."

"No, not millions," I said and laughed.

"Do you know Alexander Grant, the manager of the Kimberley Bank in Broome?" Tom asked.

"I don't think so. Not knowingly. I'm not with them anyway."

"He's a player and might be able to sort you out, but he'll want a golden handshake for his efforts. I can ask him if you're interested."

"How do you know this shit? How do you know he's in the game?"

"I taught him."

A week later Tommy pulled out paperwork with the Kimberley Bank letterhead all over it.

"We need to go through this Kat and sort out some details, like what name you want to use. You need to start practicing a signature in that name that you can handle easily if someone is watching."

"How much is this going to cost me?"

"A grand."

With a little sarcasm in my voice I said, "He's not shy then?"

"Be happy that I didn't put my percentage on the top or it would have doubled. He's taking a risk and he retires later in the year. He's just putting some cream on the top before he bails out."

"Why haven't you put your hand out?"

"I'm happy Kat. You let me hang out here away from my missus all week and you fill me up with piss every Friday. I reckon we're square on the deal."

On another occasion, again with a few beers under his belt, he would tell me about the biggest win he had while working as a bank manager.

Unusual, for it was early on a Friday afternoon and all the labourers, contractors and hanger-on's had shot through. We had the most important table in the business, the outside 'smoko' table, to ourselves. Shaded by two very old palm trees, slightly out of view from the main road and considered to be the boardroom of the business. Or businesses plural to be more precise.

This table was my 'happy place'. And I really didn't give a rat's arse if anyone shared that view with me or not. My business, my yard, my table, my palm trees, blue sky, warm weather enveloping my body and my other best friend in the entire world was buried 20 metres away between the two big bougainvillea that grew down the perimeter mesh fence. I could see his resting place from my side of the table. King, my 12-year-old German shepherd.

On many occasions, when I had the pleasure of my own company, I'd sit at that table thinking of King and the times we had swam off Gantheaume Point together and when he'd sit on the rocky outcrop up to his neck, watching me snorkelling the reef nearby. Christ, I loved that animal.

Tommy snapped me back to the conversation. "Remember the seven-year itch scam I told you about?" he asked.

"Yep."

"Well, I was in on a ripper one years ago."

"Hang on a minute, let me get another couple of beers, I reckon I might enjoy this." As I got up, I wiped moisture from my eyes, a hangover from reminiscing about King. With a bit of luck, Tommy would have interpreted it as sweat.

"When the Vietnam War was in full swing, late sixties, early seventies, the Yanks were pouring a lot of money into Australia for a variety of reasons. Might have been to pay wages, pay for upgrades to Australian Government infrastructure, paying off the fucking wharfies to dock ships without interference, commodities like fuel and food, a million things.

"Most of the legitimate dough went through genuine accounts but no one will ever know where or by who, clandestine accounts were established all over the place for Christ only knows why.

"Knowing what I know now, there must have been hundreds of them.

"Anyway, Australia pulled out of Vietnam in 1970, the Yanks hung on for another five years, keeping in mind that they had been there since 1955.

"But back before all of that, back in the late sixties, '67 to be precise, I'd been keeping my eye on a few seven-year itch accounts. One had a hundred and ninety-eight grand in it and was showing up without ever having had a transaction take place on it. Not so much as to buy a round of beers or a pie and sauce had ever been withdrawn from it.

"Have you any idea how much two hundred large was worth around 1967?"

"No idea," I admitted. "Double, triple in today's dollars?"

"A shit load, Kat. You could have brought ten suburban houses with that sort of dough.

"So, this was really unusual and smelled like dirty money to me. Who plonks nearly $200k into an account and walks away? Either a crook that's in jail or a crook that died, right?"

Tommy had me glued to my chair. "Yeah, keep going".

"I took a drive to check out the address on the account which was only about a mile from the bank. It turned out to be an office block next door to the American Consulate in St Kilda Road. It sure as hell wasn't a suburban house owned by some old granny. I ran my eyes over the brass plaques down the side of the double glass doors and nothing matched the name on the account. It was all white-collar businesses, accountants, solicitors, couple of shipping agents, shit like that. I wasn't about to go banging on any doors there, but it hinted to me that the account was crooked anyway. My best guess was a dodgy solicitor's office or something along those lines. I pulled in a partner, shifty prick I had used previously and did a deal for a sixty – forty split with him.

"I sorted out the signature card exchange using the partner's alias and had a new passbook created with the blue-light signature verification inside the back cover.

"With six months to go on the seven-year forfeit, we started hitting it.

"We planned it well in that he'd go country and pull-out dough in towns where there was a horse race meeting on that day. A good conversation piece to have with the bank teller that he was going to plonk a dollar on a horse or was in town to buy one, shit like that.

"He'd hit a bank that was opposite a car yard, 'Just need some cash to get a better deal on that car over there'. Always had a back-up story.

"He walked into a variety of suburban branches on a Friday lunchtime when everyone was flat out and couldn't care less what you wanted to do with your eight or nine grand withdrawals.

"It took months to clear the account out, right down to the last two dollars.

"I replaced the authentic signature card and burnt the passbook.

"It was a great sting except… A month short of the original seven-year expiry date, a junior teller was confronted by a Yank with a fucking cowboy hat on. He came into the branch to give notice that he would pick up the $198k in cash later in the week and close the account. It had to be cash, he wasn't interested in a bank cheque. Asks if we would make sure the funds were available.

"It was a common practice to be given prior notice of large cash withdrawals. You would have to have been a very large branch to be carrying two hundred grand above the daily requirements back then.

"The teller did the right thing and confirmed the Yank's identity, matching the signature card with the passbook he had presented with and they matched perfectly.

"But he became a little upset when he was told that he was mistaken, that there was only two dollars in the account.

"An internal audit took place but nobody, including me, could offer up an explanation.

"The Australian Federal Police got dragged in and interviewed everyone in the branch.

"By the time they got to me, I was sweating a bit, but calm and clean. The only thing that could point to me was if my fingerprints had been on the signature card. Well of course they would be, along with fifty other people, tellers, auditors and coppers.

"They grilled me for an entire day and I learnt more from them than they did from me.

"All the withdrawal slips had been gathered up and laid out in front of me. All showed the same signature scribble from my shifty partner. Then they asked me if I recognised the name or signature. No, I did not, I said.

"The only description they had of the fraudster was that he was about this height and about that age. Very vague. Obviously, I had no idea who that could be.

"They knew it had to be an inside job but also knew only twenty people with the background knowledge and balls to do it, could have been responsible. Then they asked if I had any suspicions towards any staff members, past or present. Again I told them, no, I did not.

"Was I aware the account was an American government account, registered to the Central Intelligence Agency and that the funds were related to support of the American war effort in Vietnam?

"That sat me back in my seat. I allowed myself to sound shocked. No, I was unaware of that." Tom ended with a chuckle.

"What did you do with the dough?" I asked.

"Dripped it away over twenty years, really small purchases. Filling the car up with fuel, groceries, few beers, occasional counter lunch, ten-dollar lottery tickets. No flash cars or holidays mate, that's the secret. A dickhead would go on a spending spree, buy a car, a nice mink coat for his wife, couple of new suits, dumb stuff. The minute one person says, 'He's doing alright for himself,' you just put a huge target on your back."

"Your wife knows?"

"Might have suspected early on, but no. The subject has never come up."

"The partner?"

"Coppers got him about ten years later driving through New South Wales with a boot full of marijuana. He did a bit of time for that, but no, he was never spoken to about President Johnston's dough."

I leant over and patted him on the back. "You shifty fucker Tom, well done."

I was fascinated that this retired gentleman, pillar of society, sitting in front of me out under a palm tree in the stinking heat, with a beer in his hand and sweat dripping off his nose was a polished and successful crook.

You can look people in the eye and think you know them or have an understanding of their character but it's not necessarily the case.

What's the expression? "Never judge a book by its cover."

The Helicopter Pilot

One of the Roof Plumber's mates was a legend of the area who had been tagged as 'Cowboy' long before we ever met him. So that's how the Plumber introduced him to Dodger.

Cowboy was looking to expand his own second income and was chasing powder.

He was an interesting character, worked as a helicopter mustering pilot flying Robinson-22s throughout the Kimberley. Living the dream, working on the desert fringe, being paid to throw a helicopter around like he was driving a Mini Cooper.

He had a reputation as being a very good pilot but also and probably the main reason for his nickname, a bit of a cowboy. Kimberley folklore told that no one had ever been game enough to ride in the second seat beside him. To be honest, if he was on the gear and wired while turning the helicopter inside out, you couldn't have blamed them.

He had been freelancing between several stations and we knew he took helicopters into either Broome or Kununurra for servicing, depending on which town was closest to the station he was working for. He also had a part-time job; moving dope around the top end.

The Plumber had briefed us that he had been moving a heap of our Gunja for some time, which helped answer part of the question about where all the dope was going to.

His first purchase of powder was made directly through Dodger for one ounce. Standard procedure when you're trying to ascertain, "who's who in the zoo." If it worked out, we'd make the Plumber deal to him and Dodger and I would step back into the shadows.

That first ounce of white must have got the thumbs up with whoever was into it at his end and he was chasing us within a couple of days wanting four more as soon as possible. We handed him off to the Plumber and in the weeks that followed four went to six went to eight. Half a pound at a time. That sort of quantity wouldn't have been going to station hands unless they were sprinkling it over their Wheaties. It was quite obvious to us that he had access to movers and shakers in the towns he frequented.

Due to his profession and freedom of movement, he would have had good contacts in every town through the north-west, easy access and a half respectable job that wouldn't have raised any suspicion.

Freight was a little tricky as he couldn't just jump in a helicopter and claim he needed to take it to Broome every week for servicing.

There were regulations requiring the choppers to have the engine and airframe serviced and inspected after every one-hundred hours of flight time but very few in Cowboy's industry took any notice of that. However, it did give him a legitimate excuse if he needed one and he did manage to pull it on a few times, which meant they would have been the best maintained helicopters in Australia back then.

There were a couple of freight companies who were running direct services from Broome to the cattle stations and we used them as a last resort. We would pack up a variety of old fridge motors or crap we had laying around, wrap and strap them so that they looked important and marked it up to his attention.

He told us about a banger ute he owned and the mag wheels we used with Pablo finished up on it, after the half pound had been removed from inside the tire.

I quite liked the bloke, not only for the colour of his money but his character had a fair bit of bluff and bluster about it that appealed to me. The sort of bloke that could have sold sand to the Arabs, or he would have been perfectly at home selling second-hand cars.

Outside of the helicopter he always wore a cowboy hat. I never figured out if that was another reason for his nickname or he wore it to compliment it. Either way, he wore it well and it suited him.

He flagged a quick lunch meeting with us to, 'iron out some fine detail'. He was only in Broome for the day and was busy running around for his real job. Dodger and I were full gas with our own stuff, so we had all agreed on two beers, a quick bite, one hour and back to work.

When we arrived at the Tavern Sports Bar, he was seated with half an inch of his pint missing, so he hadn't been there long.

"You ordered lunch?" Dodger asked him.

"Yeah. Sorted, thanks."

Dodger swung around to me, "What you having, Kat?"

"You paying? Beauty. The lunch special mate, pint and steak sanga, thanks."

I pulled the seat out opposite Cowboy. "What's up?" I asked.

"Wait a sec till Dodger sits down so nothing gets misunderstood."

Now this sounded a bit serious, the tone of his voice and his body language suggested a problem and the hair on the back of my neck was standing up. He was clearly not interested in idle chat.

I looked back over my shoulder to see where Dodger was, hoping he wasn't going to be long. This time of the year was starting to get busy with tourists and grey nomads, but the place was unusually quiet and Dodger had two beers being placed in front of him.

I made an attempt to break the uncomfortable silence, "We got a problem?"

"Wait," Cowboy said in an authoritative tone that was intended to shut me up.

"Fucking settle Sunshine, we're on the same team here."

"I'm not sure about that," he replied.

Thank Christ, Dodger arrived and plonked two beers on the table. Before he had time to pull out his seat, Cowboy cut to the chase. "We need to agree on who buys from who and you blokes don't sell anything into Kununurra."

"More information mate, what are ya talking about?" I asked, knowing that Dodger was oblivious to the attitude that was being offered up.

"There would be things you blokes don't know about. Like the main player in Kununurra, his name is 'Rocket'. He owns a takeaway food joint, buys a shit load of green off me and since I found you blokes, he's been taking most of the white as well."

He was right, we didn't know about this and it was probably none of our business anyway.

"So, where's the problem?" Dodger asked.

"The fucking problem, Dodger…" Cowboy said, staring Dodger down and pointing his finger at him, "Is that when the Plumber was working in Kununurra a couple of weeks back he bypassed me and flogged off ounces to Rocket and half a boot full of green. Caused me some grief, undercutting the shit out of my prices. He's a prick, he knew Rocket was my contact and he's gone in there to chop my legs off. Now he can get fucked. I know he gets the green off you blokes, he told me that."

"He shouldn't be spreading stories like that," Dodger said with considerable sarcasm in in his voice.

"That's your problem, not mine. So, in future, if you want to keep doing business, I only buy off you two. Gunja and powder. How you compensate the Plumber is up to you. I don't give a fuck about him."

I jumped in, "Keep your voice down."

"It's gotta be less stressful for me and you, to have one point of contact than me dealing with the three of you, especially when the Plumber isn't always in town and you're the fucking supplier anyway.

"Rocket reckons he can move a shit load more, but I want a guarantee that the three of you don't sell a fucking bean into Kununurra."

He had a good point but there were a couple of grey areas to sort out. "Yeah, fair call. We can pull the Plumber out of Kununurra. He's only doing odd jobs there, he spends most of his life over this side anyway. We can sort that.

"And yes, you buy whatever you need directly off Dodger, he's your contact from today. We have an arrangement with the Plumber on Gunja sales, so he won't miss out. Only problem is that he was well entrenched into Derby and Fitzroy Crossing, long before you arrived," I added.

"I don't give a fuck about them, he can do what he wants there. I've got a couple of contacts there but our paths wont cross. Just keep him out of the big K."

"So, we're cool then?" Dodger asked as he looked around to see where our steak sandwiches were.

"If we all agree, then we are. Let's get back to making some money then hey?"

The crisis was avoided with simple negotiation. However, it was a reminder to me that there was a big difference and a gulf of a divide between good, legitimate business protocols and the ethics of drug dealers whose only concern was greed. In hindsight, Dodger and I had the skills of both.

The Plumber had a slightly different version of the story in that he had a weeks' worth of work pre-arranged in Kununurra. He'd loaded up his ute with product on the assumption that he'd sell it off to his contacts in Derby, Fitzroy Crossing and Hall's Creek on his way to Kununurra. He told us that he hadn't had as much success as he had banked on, either because he couldn't find his people or they weren't in town or some other fuck around. I didn't really give a shit.

Either way, he didn't want to be driving around all week up there or back across the top end with a shit load of gear on him.

To ease his stress level, he went and spoke to Rocket, who he admitted he knew through Cowboy anyway and sold him everything he had on board.

We accepted the Plumber's version as we would have done exactly the same thing but gave him the heads up that Kununurra was now out of bounds.

The Cowboy was fairly reliable, as far as our contacts went, but he lived life on the edge sometimes. I wasn't sure if he liked it or just didn't think things through. On one of his trips he radioed Brisbane Air Traffic Control. It was an Aussie quirk that because Broome's tower was only manned part-time, anyone flying out during those quiet hours still had to seek permission to take off and therefore the radio call was handled by Brisbane. I always wondered at that. It would be the equivalent of a crop-duster helicopter pilot radioing Los Angeles International Airport to give him permission to take off from some shit-kicking airstrip in Hillbilly Creek, Kentucky. But that's the way ATC Australia-style worked.

With a flight plan that would have taken him back to the station where the helicopter lived, Cowboy took off from runway 28 and rose gently with the nose facing west.

At five hundred feet, he remembered he'd forgotten something, so he changed course and instead of doing a 180 degree left turn out over Gantheaume Point, he swung the helicopter to the north and tracked visually towards the Divers Tavern. He radioed in that he suspected a mechanical problem and advised that he would land at the designated helipad opposite the Divers Tavern.

Brisbane ATC acknowledged and because they considered it an emergency, notified the Broome coppers who sent a car out to assist.

When the cops arrived, the blades were still turning in idle with Cowboy standing outside of the rotor radius. He told the coppers it was all sorted, it was only a loose luggage door and asked them if they'd mind keeping any spectators away while he just ran over the road to use the toilet at the Tavern.

The coppers were okay with that.

They would have had kittens if they knew there was half a pound of amphetamine and two pounds of Gunja packed into the luggage locker.

When Cowboy returned five minutes later, he was carrying a carton of beer over his shoulder that he strapped into the passenger seat, telling the cops, "Present for my boss."

He belted up, advised Brisbane he was taking off again, waved to the cops and flew away.

The luggage door story was fantasy, he just needed a cool drink for the trip back.

Saturday Courthouse Market Day

It was a nightmare trying to find a car park space anywhere near the Courthouse on Market Day as there were thousands of additional tourists in town. We finally found a spot a couple of hundred metres away behind the post office and walked up.

The market was full of families and tourists walking around buying three-dollar sunglasses, cheap and nasty Broome T-shirts and manhandling some of the locally made artefacts. Well, locally made if the 'Made in China' sticker had been removed.

It was a pleasant enough atmosphere with a female singer and her guitarist boyfriend knocking out a few tunes in the courtyard and all the kids in front of them showing off their dance routines. A change of aroma in the air as we walked past the tents and food stalls selling coffee, satay sticks, hamburgers and fresh bread reminded me I hadn't had breakfast.

We stopped to buy a coffee and a donut, lingering, chatting to a couple of people we knew from around the place. A warm, casual, social environment.

We had a shop awning to measure up and replace in China Town but had agreed to make use of a lazy Saturday morning to walk through the markets on our way, looking like the honourable citizens we were.

As per our normal weekend routine we had no drugs on us, none in the car, none in our residences, no one looking for us.

Cleanskins.

One of the first people we ran into at the coffee van was flowerpot man Ben, trying to juggle three cups of coffee. "What are you doing here?" asked Dodger.

"Ah, we often run a stall here. Over there." Pointing with his head so he didn't lose the coffees. "Come on over. The dragons usually man it so we can keep the shop open, but we decided to open late today and crank it here with all the fucking tourists in town. We usually do okay out of it and move a bit of your gear while we're here."

We all laughed and I wondered if they called their wives 'dragons' to their face. I knew the women. I doubted it.

"But listen, I've been thinking about you blokes," he continued.

"This'll be good," Dodger said with a smirk, "Go on."

"You know anyone in the jewellery trade?"

It was my turn. "Why? What the fuck you into now?"

"You read about those pearl panels that got pinched, write up in the local newspaper?"

"You mean those things that hang in the water with pockets of pearl shells in them?" Dodger asked.

"Yeah," Ben nodded. "So do you know about them?"

Dodger shook his head, but I said, "Actually, I know a bit about it."

"For fuck's sake, Kat. Don't tell me you were in on it?" Ben's eyes widened and I thought he was going to drop his coffee.

"Not quite. I was snorkelling off Gantheaume Point a month back and found about a dozen panels off the reef. All empty. Had to have been stolen. I pulled the tags off them and gave them to one of the pearl divers that lives next door. Couple of days later the cops rang me to ask exactly where I'd found them. What's your side of the story?"

"Well…" Ole Ben was thinking about how much info he wanted to offer up, I could read it on his face.

"I know the blokes that knocked 'em off, but they're hot and so are the pearls. I'm babysitting them. The pearls, not the blokes. Gotta get rid of them, but I don't know anyone in the trade."

"Neither do I," I said, looking to Dodger but he just shook his head in reply.

"How many you got?" I asked.

"There's a small jeweller's bag full of them, about thirty I guess, maybe more, different sizes."

"What sort of dough you looking at?"

"Mate's rates, say thirty k?"

"Ain't going to happen. We'll give you six ounces of white, you'll turn that into twenty, easy."

"Fuck you Kat, they're worth thousands more than that."

"And you can't get rid of them. Only offer you're gunna get mate, take it or leave it."

As we walked back to his stall, Dodger whispered in my ear, "What the fuck are we gonna do with twenty k's worth of pearls."

I gave him a grin.

"What now, ya shifty cunt?"

"Don't panic Dodge, me ole mate. That pearl diver I turned the panels over to?"

"Yeah, what about him?"

"He told me the pearls they'd had in them were worth between 75 and 100k."

"Well fuck me."

"I'd rather shake your hand, Dodger."

After our conversation with Ben had concluded, we took a casual stroll up Hamersley Street heading towards Napier Terrace. I looked across and could see the frown on Dodger's face.

"What's up?"

"You're a shifty prick hey. What were you doing floating around off Gantheaume Point anyway? You told me you weren't going out there again 'cause of the sharks."

"Changed my mind."

"I think you're a fucking shark, Kat. I saw a couple of those panels in the back of your ute. Coincidence?"

"What, you think I was involved? I brought them home to dry them out, paint 'em and hang 'em on the verandah wall like everyone else in Broome does."

"You have a happy knack of being wherever the action is," he said with a grin, so I knew he wasn't having a crack at me.

"How you going to turn pearls into cash anyway?"

"Honestly, I have no idea, but I'll think of something. I know a jeweller in Perth who I reckon is shady… maybe." I was thinking on my feet. "Either way it's got potential, we'll make a quid on it, surely?"

"Yeah, I'm not."

"Not what?"

"Sure."

"Do you want me to just square you for the wholesale price of the gear?" I asked. I knew we always had the rider over each other. We only did things jointly that we both agreed on and I hadn't exactly asked for Dodger's permission on this one.

"Yeah probably, mate," he said. "Yeah. Count me out on this one, you're on your own. I know fuck all about pearls, jewellery, or anything to do with that shit. You sort the deal out with Ben, I don't need to know anything about it." As an afterthought, he added, "The only time I had an interest in pearls was in Thailand watching some Asian chick pull a 5-metre string of them out of her arse."

"You sure it was a chick?"

"Aww fuck off, Kat. You just spoilt that happy memory for me. Twat."

"My pleasure. I'll sort this one on my 'Pat'".

As we crossed Frederick Street, we started to hear screaming.

That unmistakable hi-pitched scream that the indigenous community do so well when engaged in conflict.

The volume has the ability to cross borders.

Now, Dodger wasn't the most racist person in the world, but it would be fair to say that he didn't tolerate drunken, violent, uncouth, loud, obnoxious behaviour very well, regardless of skin colour.

He easily took offence to rough as guts foul language being screeched out on full volume, especially in the middle of the day when kids were running around and life was meant to be surrounded by a family atmosphere.

Another reason for his unease was due to a flogging he had received a few years back that he'd never quite recovered from.

He had been working as a welder on a four-kilometre freshwater tunnel being blasted through the Darling Scarp to connect the then new Wungong Dam to the existing Perth water supply near Byford.

Some of the miners on the Friday afternoon shift had a habit of jumping in the work utes at smoko and driving down to the Narrogin Inn for a couple of pints. The theory was good but in practice, two beers lead to four or whatever they could bang in before they had to be back before shift change.

Dodger and three other blokes jumped in a ute, still fully fitted out in gum boots, filthy overalls, cap lamp battery attached to their hip and helmets slung over their shoulders. The intention was that they wouldn't be long.

A few beers later in the front bar, a bit of a shit fight started between some local indigenous guys and other local patrons. The miners got involved but only to separate the shit heads and throw a couple out the front door, then they returned to the bar.

An hour or so later they decided they really should go back to work, some five kilometres up the Albany highway at the bottom of Wungong Dam. Downing the last of their beers they headed off across the hotel car park.

They were jumped on before they had reached the dual cab, outnumbered three to one. Dodger would say they had no way of being able to put up much resistance due in part to the beer on board and the cumbersome equipment they were still hooked up too.

He never forgot the colour of the skinny legs that had been trying to kick his head in.

Back in Broome, a drunk as a skunk indigenous man was sitting on a heavy-duty wooden table, anchored in concrete, screaming and swearing as best you will ever hear.

His 'lady friend' was ten metres away, standing in a shop doorway giving it back to him at equal decibels. It was a grossly offensive and embarrassing performance.

As usual, there wasn't a copper in sight. They seemed to have an unwritten rule to ignore this shit and to keep driving by if they were in the vicinity. It avoided being tied up all day sorting out the paperwork and having to deal with legal aid banging on the front door of the police station. To be fair, the end result would amount to a complete waste of time and resources, so their best course of action was to ignore it. Let the locals sort it out.

Dodger and my direction of travel was going to take us directly behind the bloke at arm's reach.

As we got closer, I sensed Dodger's discomfort and knew from history that he was likely to get involved. I knew it was going to go to shit. I did wonder, at times like this, why I didn't turn around. Because it was Dodger, I guess. Where he went, I went. Where I went, he went. With mates, you just gotta do what you gotta do.

The screamer was delivering a crescendo when he stopped mid-word. For not the first time in his tirade he had been in the middle of explaining to his doorway friend that she resembled sexually active female genitalia. It was like she hadn't grasped it the first time. I figured he was only trying to be thorough in his explanation.

She was looking the wrong way and didn't see Dodger slam the bloke's head, face first, into the bench's plank top. When she did look back, she would have assumed her man had fallen asleep.

Fair chance he would have woken up a minute or two later in a pool of blood with his nose twice as wide as it had been and thinking that the horrific headache he was suffering was due to the four litres of cask wine he had drunk since eight o'clock that morning.

Skylab could have landed on his head for all he knew.

Others in the street must have seen what happened, but no one said a word, not a squeak. All were peacefully quiet.

As was the street.

Without missing a step, Dodger continued to walk up to Napier Terrace and hung a right past the chicken joint and onto China

Town. I followed, with a quick glance over my shoulder just to ensure all was well.

A few days earlier I'd had a desperate call from a swimsuit shop owner who said a wayward car had taken out a corner post of his bullnose verandah. It was hanging down in the street and he was desperate to have it propped up and secured.

I grabbed one of our labourers, put a couple of roof props in the ute and drove in to help the guy out. It took less than an hour to get it back up and secured with a few ropes. Not great, but it would do until a more permanent replacement across the full length of the shop front could be arranged. The owner was rapt that anyone in Broome would be so obliging and could not thank me enough.

It was going to be an insurance job and he was more than happy to fiddle with the claim in that we organised three quotes between us, loaded the job to the hilt and won it. So here we were, measuring it up.

I spotted KGB pull up and park her car on the opposite side of the road. She really was an outstanding specimen, the sight of her had my heart rate rise that high I could feel it jumping out of my chest.

Being that her office was only three doors up, the assumption was that she was going into work. She saw me and gave a little wave, got out of her car and walked around to the passenger side.

She was looking across the roof of her car staring at me. I translated the look to mean, 'I'll be here for the next fifteen seconds if you want to talk'.

I told Dodger to pretend he knew what he was doing with a tape measure in his hand and that, "I'll be back in a minute."

When I walked around to the passenger side of her car, a few things became very obvious. First, she was still the most appealing female I'd ever had my arms around. Second, she was upset and wasn't hiding it very well. Third, she had the figure to get away with wearing tight fitting clothing, but something wasn't quite right. She had either had a very big breakfast, or she was pregnant.

I remember thinking to myself, 'and if you needed confirmation that the relationship was over, there it is'.

She was standing at a distance that two people meeting in the street would do but, the magnet dragging us across that gap was difficult for both of us and it closed as the conversation progressed. She had mist in her eyes and didn't try to wipe it away.

"I'm so sorry Kat."

"Sorry for what? You don't owe me an apology for anything."

"Another time, another life, another place, I love you Kat, but it just can't be."

"We've been through this, I understand, I love you too."

An uneasy silence followed so I tried to lift the cloud a little.

"Congratulations," I said, staring at her belly.

There is a feminine side to me in that I have an uncontrollable urge to put my hand on a pregnant woman's stomach. It's not sexual and it's not a fetish. The thought of a child growing in there makes me feel all warm and fuzzy, but I had to remind myself that we were standing almost nose to nose in the main street of Broome. It would be best that I didn't cup her unborn child in my hand right now.

"Thank you," she replied and tears rolled down both her cheeks.

"What brought this on?" I asked.

"Just having a bad day and seeing you has cracked me. Sorry, Kat." She dabbed her eyes with a tissue she'd had balled up in her hand. "I need to go. Look after yourself, *Mon Chat.*" She lowered her head and let out a petite sob, turned and walked away.

Back across the road and Dodger looked up from a note pad he had been writing in, "How's she going?"

"Don't fucking ask."

***

Ten days later we had arranged to meet the insurance assessor on site so we would all be on the same page as to how the swimsuit shop job would be carried out and who was responsible for what.

A fortyish guy who was morbidly obese, levered himself out of his car and shuffled along the footpath to greet us. He was dressed neat and tidy with a pressed white shirt that could have been used as a two-man tent. Partly because of the stifling humidity but more to do with his health, by the time he walked the forty metres to us, he needed to steady himself against the verandah post and the nice white shirt was saturated.

He introduced himself, "I'm Frank. We spoke on the phone. You guys would be Kat and Dodger, hey?"

Our brand new khaki work shirts with our names on the right-hand side of the chest and our business name and logo on the left might have hinted that he had that right.

The official meeting lasted three minutes. With a bit of hand waving and building gibberish, 'we'll do this, we'll do that, it'll take five days' was about the extent of the conversation.

"We need to get out of the fucking heat," Frank said, sweat pissing out of every wrinkle of his body.

"The bar's next door, you feel like a beer?" Dodger asked him.

"Excellent fuckin' idea," he replied with a fair amount of enthusiasm.

The bloke was that big he had to spread his arse over two chairs. I sat opposite and Dodger came back from the bar with three beers. Before we had taken a sip, fat Frank had skulled his pint. Dodger raised his eyebrows and pushed his untouched beer across the table to him.

"Here, get into this. You should have said you were thirsty!"

With that, Dodger returned to the bar and sorted out another beer for himself and a jug for Frank.

We spent a couple of hours pouring grog into our new acquaintance to learn that he wasn't all that interested in his job, as long as he got paid every Friday he couldn't care less. His main concern was that he had access to a pub lunch, a gut's full of beer and fifty bucks in his back pocket to pay for his next head job. If all that was in order, then he was living the dream.

As the afternoon progressed and the more grog he took on, (three to our one) he loosened up in our company enough to feed into the conversation that he could use a joint or two to unwind with for the afternoon. Did we know anywhere he could lay his hands on some?

Dodger dropped the acid straight on him, "I can sort you some green. I know people who have some, but talk us through what other work you have up here that we could get a piece of?"

Dodger's thought process was that we might be able to up the quote or load up a few extras on the swimsuit shop job. Frank's reply was either a con or a very generous offer.

"Sort some dope every time I come to town and you win whatever job I'm signing off on. That'd be a fair deal, wouldn't it? Maybe a few beers as well?" he added.

We'd heard he carried a bit of weight, so to speak, with insurance jobs and he'd just sold his arse for a bag of dope and some beers. Dodger and I nodded at each other and my partner in crime disappeared for three minutes to retrieve half an ounce he just happened to have in the glove box of the ute.

Big Boy was rapt that he'd found a couple of blokes he could work with that would fuel him up with grog and an ounce of marijuana in exchange for a few insurance jobs. The relationship went very well for us and he must have directed four hundred grand's worth of work our way in the couple of years that followed. He would get word to us of jobs that had come up on his radar, then ring us to give us the heads up on who, if anyone, was quoting and what figure would win the job. He was sharp enough to never put any shifty stuff in writing.

Some of the prime jobs came when no one else in town was interested and he would tell us to load it up. Our piss-ant expenses propping him up and letting him think we were the best mates he ever had, returned us thousands of extra legitimate dollars in profit.

Broome Races

In August of '94, a mate of ours was running the bars at the Broome Races and was under the pump to find staff for the finale of the season, Broome Cup Day.

The Broome Race Round is a series of race days put on by the Turf Club between May and August each year, climaxing with the Broome Cup Day on the Saturday. A Ladies Day happens the following Tuesday but most of Broome are still suffering from hangovers, so it's not as well attended.

Everyone in Broome wants to be at Cup Day but most of them wouldn't know what a horse looks like. A learned person might say that it has a leg in each corner and that would be the extent of their equine knowledge.

The interest in being there is that it is a unique day out on Gantheaume Point. Warm to hot weather, blazing sunshine, red pindan dirt squeaking like powder between your toes, loud music, well-dressed women and alcohol. Lots of alcohol. And, did I mention, there are some horse races on as well.

Every man, woman or child that lives in the Kimberley and who has a touch of Aussie heritage in them, plus a couple of thousand overseas backpackers and half of Australia's grey nomad population all want to be there.

Our mate asked me and Dodger if we knew anyone that might be interested or if we'd help out and work behind the bar for Cup Day. He was desperate for staff and more desperate for people he could trust. Dodger declined, he wanted to pull on a new shirt, shave up, put his best thongs on and play up.

I decided it would be a good day out, something different and offered to work. I didn't need the two hundred bucks on offer, the bloke had sent a bit of construction work our way previously, so I figured I could return the favour. I thought it would be entertaining being on the other side of the bar for a change. He did warn me that it might be a bit hectic. That turned out to be a massive fucking understatement.

Patrons wanting a drink would buy 'tickets' from a separate tent that handled the cash. One ticket brought you a can of soft drink, two tickets a can of beer, three tickets a can of pre-mixed drink, like Bourbon and Coke. All aluminium cans, no glass. The punters lined up at one of the bars and purchased their desired beverage, handing over the appropriate number of tickets. Easy.

Now, I'm no accountant but I can add up. I looked up a few times at the cash tent and saw how that was going and saw firsthand how the grog and ticket transfer went down. I'd like someone to try and explain to me how that balanced at the end of the night. I'm glad it wasn't my job.

There were twenty staff working, 'my bar' and it was the most full-on, intense, ten hours of work in my life. Five deep along the length of the bar all day, people screaming orders and flicking tickets in your face. The ice troughs had to be constantly refilled with ice and a variety of different drinks from the refrigerator containers out the back. It was a stinking hot day and the compressor on the container wasn't worth a cold pie. Most of the beers coming out of the container and into the trough were warm by about lunchtime, the ice troughs couldn't handle the heat and the pissheads were being served near boiling beer in the afternoon. By that stage they were so drunk they didn't notice.

I saw Dodger a couple of times during the day, but it was just a nod of recognition.

He would tell me later that it was a circus on his side of the bar. A massive party with an estimated ten thousand people rolling around the pindan, sun on their heads and grog in their guts.

He spent half his day in the two-up ring trying to top up his back-pocket there.

Hundreds of patrons circled the ring all day, forming their own little groups and betting off each other. It must be one of the most simplistic forms of gambling. I mean how hard is throwing two coins in the air and guessing what way they'll land, but it's unique to Australia, a legacy to our ANZAC heritage and, oh yeah, illegal. Other than on ANZAC Day itself. Broome Races are not on ANZAC Day. No one seemed to mind.

The government had tried to get its claws into some of the two-up money and had allowed a single venue, the Crown Casino in Perth, to have a licensed form of it. I was fairly sure Broome Races weren't being held in there either. Again, no one seemed to mind.

It's none of my business and I'm the last bloke that is going to stop a police officer and ask him if he's comfortable that five hundred people are over the back playing two-up but how does that work? What government official, politician or regional police inspector says, "Don't worry about it, look the other way, all day."

Next time I get pulled over for speeding, I'm going to try that on, "Officer, today is a speed-free day."

Dodger had seen all of our major customers, legit ones and the ones moving the gear. The ones making the big dollar on the day had been making multiple trips to the car park to retrieve more stock to flog off to the bottom feeders. A couple of them approached Dodger to ask if he had any more on him and he told them to fuck off. He'd told all of them during the week to order what they needed on the Friday as he wasn't on call over the weekend. A little side issue was that we had been cleaned out anyway, we didn't have a skerrick stashed anywhere. Our next, 'fridge' wasn't due in till the following Tuesday and that would be if the semi was on schedule. The dickheads would learn one way or another that Dodger was good to his word and endorsed by me.

We estimated that two pounds of amphetamine supplied by us went through Broome that weekend. We made more money than any punter did and didn't get our hands dirty in the process.

Late in the shift I spotted KGB fighting her way to the front of the bar with the advantage of a now sizeable bump. She was stunning as usual and it warmed my heart to lay eyes on her again. I made a beeline for her.

She did a double take, surprised to see me at all, let alone on my side of the bar. She pulled on one of those sultry smiles that only a tipsy woman that sights an ex-lover can display. Being that I was the ex-lover, she had me in the palm of her hands. I did wonder about her drinking in her condition, but perhaps the rules for that were relaxed on Race Day as much as those around two-up. Who was I to judge?

She made that two handed, 'come closer' gesture used in bars and night clubs when you cannot hear a fucking thing and someone wants to speak to you.

I fell for it hook, line and sinker. The floor of my side of the bar was slightly lower than the patron's side so I had to lean over the beer troughs with both my hands on the counter and bend over. She grabbed hold of my head, pulled me towards her and delivered the most magnificent, sweet, full lipped, alcohol-laden kiss. Holding it, I sensed her tongue flicking over my teeth and moving deeper. She may have caught me off guard, but I recovered well, letting her know through my own proactive response that I wasn't offended.

There were fifty screaming patrons either side of us at the bar, none of them gave a rat's arse about the embrace; they just wanted drinks.

KGB eventually released her grip, probably to breathe and ordered two drinks. I've no idea what I handed her or if I took her tickets. She gave me a wink and disappeared into the crowd.

I spent the remainder of the shift with a twinge in my groin, wondering if I needed to trim the bougainvillea.

The Pommy Nurse

Now, throughout your life you will be exposed to life-changing events that will change your direction. I call these events, 'fate'. Others might see them as 'good luck' or 'bad luck' events. It depends on the circumstances.

A change of work roles that you choose would be fate because you chose this direction or that direction. You probably wouldn't reflect on it until years later and only then recognise it as a life-changing event.

The sudden death of a loved one would be catastrophic and instant. You would recognise that immediately as a bad luck event and that it would have the potential to direct your life one way or another.

A lottery win or picking up an inheritance that opened up some freedom for you might be seen as a good luck event.

You're driving along an open road, tapping your fingers to the music on the radio, in a split second the car coming towards you is in the gravel, it overcorrects and is heading your way. You didn't see it coming and the reflex time was zero. If he missed you by an inch then you had a good day. The alternative could have been life-changing. That's fate.

The point of all this is that you never know when your life will change. It will come out of the blue, you won't see it coming or have planned it. Unexplained and without warning, a click of the fingers and your life is shunted down a different train line.

***

When the bar shift finished at the races, the staff were invited to have, 'staffies' around a few bench seats in the open area. The dust had settled, the noise had disappeared and the patrons had staggered off. Some of the die-hards were kicking on in a handful of the car park parties but they weren't our concern anymore. All the staff were rooted and needed two things, a seat and a drink.

I parked myself down with a beer in each hand, I knew the first one wouldn't touch the sides, so I'd grabbed two. It would save me getting up again for five minutes.

Sitting beside me was a sweet, slim, young, blonde, attractive female with a Pommy accent and a set of 34C breasts. Cute little thing with a sense of humour. She had been working my bar all day and we had had some brief working-related conversations so we knew each other.

The cleavage she had on display didn't offend my eyes either.

We enjoyed a pleasant and engaging conversation and I would learn that she had arrived in Sydney as a backpacker eight months previously. She had been tip toeing her way around Australia since. By the way she was banging in the VB's, I figured she'd gotten a handle on Australia without too much of a problem.

Because she wasn't rolling in dough and being that she was a qualified ED, an Emergency Department nurse, she had decided to apply for a job at Broome Hospital. They were screaming for qualified personnel at the time and so she was going to be staying put for a while. The role was supported by subsidised accommodation and the package suited her fine.

She picked up the bar-service job as a one-off as she wasn't rostered on at the hospital that weekend and could do with an extra couple of hundred bucks in her back pocket.

One more drink and we were given the 'let's wrap it up please guys' by the last remaining security blokes and the food and beverage supervisors. The Pom had sounded me out a bit, to be clear in her mind that I wasn't related to the Yorkshire Ripper, and asked if there was a chance she could hitch a ride back to the nurse's quarters.

"Of course, no problem."

As my ute bounced down the corrugated road out of Gantheaume Point, I suggested I needed a night cap before my head hit the pillow and asked if she was interested. My intention was totally honourable at this stage, I genuinely needed an amber-coloured hydration top up. She would not have offended me if she had said no.

"My place is only two hundred metres from the nurse's lodge, you happy we pull in there?"

"Yeah, sure," came the reply.

The evening was still, the heat had come off the day and my fridge was working exceptionally well. We sat outside and both relaxed, allowing the stress and pressure of working our guts out all day to slide away.

We had a couple of drinks. She found a bottle of Gin on the shelf above the beer fridge. I'd no idea where it came from, sure as fuck it didn't belong to me, so she gave it a nudge.

An hour later her skinny little arse was parked up in my bed, where, apart from a couple of minor hiccups, it would stay for the next twenty-five years.

Fate.

"You should enter the Wet T competition at the Roey, you'd shit it in."

"You're two weeks late mate, I already won it."

"Fair enough."

Holidays

One of the beauties of living in the Kimberley was the fact you could go just about anywhere you wanted to, do whatever you wanted to and the chance of seeing anyone else was rare.

We'd decided to drive up to Cape Leveque early on a Saturday morning with an open plan of swimming, fishing and drinking a couple of beers. We took both vehicles up, with blow-up mattresses in case we needed them, fishing gear, snorkelling masks, spear guns, a small esky full of food and a large esky full of grog.

The relationship between Dodger and his second wife had been rocky at best and she had gone back to her hometown of Adelaide for a month or two to consider their future. The main problem was that she hated Broome and wanted out. Dodger loved the place, was equal partner in a growing business and secretly enjoyed the thought of being the king of the Broome underbelly, although he couldn't exactly advertise that.

He wasn't going anywhere.

In her absence he hadn't been spending all day moping around the house watching Elvis repeats on TV. Instead he'd invited one of his pickups from the Divers Tavern, a tall, well-endowed blonde bird with a bit more character in her than his wife, to join us on the Cape Leveque trip.

The Pom wrangled the weekend off work at the hospital and I threw her in the passenger seat of my four-wheel drive. She'd been camping a couple of times before but hadn't experienced the Dodger-Kat style of roughing it in the bush yet. I was apprehensive about how she'd handle our 'no rules' behaviour, figuring that if she thought we were out of line she could always walk the two hundred kilometres back to Broome.

But I had underestimated her. Underneath the Pommy skin lay a 'I don't give a fuck, nothing rattles me, I'll do whatever I want, when I want' freedom-seeking monster.

Five minutes after we pulled up on the reed grass sand hills looking north-east towards the Timor Sea we declared, 'this is us', the esky was opened and tested, all shirts were removed and I mean all, not a bikini top had been packed.

We'd found a slightly remote bay on the northern tip of the peninsula, with our one private beach. Everything in the back of the utes had been pulled out to make way for the blow-up mattresses. Deck chairs were set up and a half-decent campfire was established from odd bits of driftwood and half an old railway sleeper we'd had at the factory.

We swam with black tipped reef sharks and watched turtles float past at arm's reach. Dodger caught a couple of Threadfin Salmon from the beach and threw them on a makeshift BBQ. We drank beer and wine and had sex, (me with the Pom, not Dodger), on the beach under a full moon.

Fuelled by alcohol, Dodger and I argued over who was the fittest and had a bet on a running race to the rocky point and back, about six hundred metres return.

"The problem with you Kat is that you think you're Muhammad Ali, Tony Lockett, Maradona, Ben Johnson and Eddy Merckx all rolled into one. The only thing you'd ever beat me in is a game of cards," he offered up.

"Really? That wouldn't be hard, the only card game you know would be 'snap'. Who's Eddy Merckx?"

"With your heritage, you've never heard of Eddy Merckx? Serious? Don't worry about it."

I looked across the flickering campfire and could see the outline of Dodger's sixpack. There was no denying he was in good nick for a bloke that drank as much grog as he did.

"I wouldn't wrestle you Dodge, I'd be frightened you'd roll on me and your fat guts would squash me." The four of us had a giggle knowing that I was talking shit.

"Okay, let's do this. No cheating, you have to touch the rock face at the other end, right?"

The Pom jumped up wanting in and declaring that she'd, "Tear our fucking legs off."

Dodger's girlfriend waved a towel as the start/finish flag.

With only the moon lighting up the sand we took off laughing, stumbling and trying to trip each other up.

The Pom was good to her word and we owed her two cartons for the win.

***

"We're going on a holiday," says Dodger.

"Your life is one big fucking holiday."

"I'm serious," he said, trying to force my attention.

"We did Cape Leveque two weeks ago," I reminded him.

"We did and it was terrific, but, I'm talking about a real holiday. We haven't had a proper holiday for two years. We have a long weekend coming up, right?"

"Yep."

"So hear me out. We're going to Bali for a few days." He was bubbling with enthusiasm.

"You serious? Why Bali? It's a dog's breakfast of a place?" I replied.

"Okay. For a start, step out of your comfort zone, Kat. You've never been there. You're like a kid telling his mother he won't eat his greens, but he's never tasted them. How would he know if he liked them or not? You're no different. Your opinion is based on what other fuckers have told you. You've never been near the joint. Right?"

He had a point. "Go on, I'm listening."

"They started flying Broome to Bali direct a month ago. There's an early flight up on Friday morning, we could be in the resort pool by midday at the latest. We swing on a few beers, do a couple of

125

tourist things, I'll take you up to Ubud, you'll love it. There's a monkey jungle place, temple thing."

"You have the tourist patter down, I see."

"Fuck off. Or we could do the beaches? Great beaches, or there's a live volcano."

"What, like Pompeii live volcano?"

"I don't know what it's called, mate."

I shook my head as he pressed on.

"Or if you're past your use-by date, you can sit in the room and watch TV all day with the aircon on full bore."

The last bit was a dig at me that he reckoned I was getting old. I couldn't help but interrupt him, "Fuck you."

He continued, "I know what you're thinking. Because it's a long weekend, what happens with the factory? Well, if the welders want to work on Saturday, Chris has keys, he can supervise. Tommy can come in if he wants to run the joint. My bet is that as Monday is the public holiday, no one will want to be here anyway.

"The other problem is the dope. We tell Bill and Ben to fuel up on Thursday because we have family coming into town and we'll be unavailable till the Tuesday. The Plumber is sorted. Cowboy said he wouldn't be back to the middle of the following week anyway and any bottom feeders can wait. We can't tell any of them we're going away because if they get too smart they might want to ransack our houses or this joint looking for dope or cash. We don't need that. They need to think we're still in town."

I jumped in, "That's a fair call. And what about the…" I left the sentence hanging, he knew I was referring to our female companions.

"Mine's only on the drip feed, she's not invited. Yours is working. I already heard her talking about it. Besides, you've only been banging her for a couple of months, this trip was booked before then. Get my drift? And you're still sulking over KGB giving you the arse, a break will do you good."

"You really are a cunt, hey? I'm not sulking."

"So we're going." He'd made the decision and I was out of the argument.

"I'll book it all tomorrow in a nice resort, two rooms because you snore."

I had a thought. "How's the bird at the travel agency going? She sell you this plan?"

I knew he was keen on a doll that worked there.

He pulled on a smirk. "You don't miss much do you? For the record, this is my idea. Give me your passport details."

***

The Dodger's plan went ahead.

There were enough checks and balances in place for the legitimate business to survive without a blimp. Tommy owned the place for three days and I doubt a single tek-screw left the premises without it being invoiced.

Dodger sorted all the drug fuckers out. Being a long weekend, Bill and Ben took most of our reserves off us, there was very little left locked away that we needed to stress about. The next delivery from Pablo wasn't due till Tuesday arvo and we planned to be back by then anyway.

Before the plane took off, I'd been thinking about the business decision to run direct flights from Broome to Bali and vice versa. I couldn't understand who would really want to travel from one of the most pristine tropical areas in the world to the same, two hours north. The only rationale could be cheap beer and satay sticks. But when I relaxed back into seat 12A, it occurred to me that a substantial amount of people on the full plane were European backpackers who had exhausted Australia and were travelling back home via Indonesia. The idea wasn't as silly as it first appeared.

There is a distinct aroma about Asia and I'm not talking about the open drains. Almost anywhere I'd been in Asia previously had a cooking fragrance in the air and Bali was no different, it greeted us as we walked out of the terminal. No idea where it was coming from, but it sure smelt good. It was my first impression and I wanted whatever it was.

However, the traffic was a shit fight. Millions of people, millions of scooters, some of which seemed to cater for a driver and an extra five people balanced precariously on the rear pillion, handlebars and wherever else they could squeeze on to. Also, no discernible road rules. Coming from Broome where there wasn't a traffic light for six hundred kilometres, this was an eye opener. And the noise! Every man and his dog had his hand on a car or scooter horn and used it as the in between activity of braking and accelerating. With two thousand taxis playing the game at the same time it was like an off-beat orchestra at full pitch that ear plugs and earmuffs wouldn't keep out of your head.

I had to compliment Dodger on the choice of accommodation he'd sorted out with his part-time girlfriend at the travel agency. The beach-front resort was magnificent. I'd never stayed in such luxurious accommodation in my life. Walking into the open-air lobby, which was bigger than most houses we'd built, took my breath away. Quality timber furniture, flowers, paintings, palm trees poking through the roof and large ceiling fans wafting cool air, was impressive. The gentle wooden tones of a little man sitting cross-legged in the open space and banging melodically on a bamboo xylophone-type instrument all added to the ambiance of the place. I was immediately relaxed.

After booking in and being shown to our spacious rooms that overlooked one of the quarter-acre swimming pools on the estate, we decided to take a walk up the main road in front of the resort to get our bearings. Maybe find a quiet bar and some of the Asian food that had been teasing our nostrils.

We'd walked about fifty metres and had been accosted twenty times by locals wanting us to buy a T-shirt, or get a special massage or be fitted for a new suit when two young, shifty-looking characters standing in a door recess, stepped out to shirt front us.

"You want good drugs, very good marijuana? We have."

"Fuck off," Dodger said to them, assuming his Australian cultural attaché status, but then he quickly had a rethink. "You have powder, speed? How much?"

I'm standing there thinking, "I hope he's not serious."

"Yes, we have very much good price you like," said one of the super salesmen, pulling out a small wad of something wrapped in alfoil. "One gram, twenty-five Aussie dollar, best speed in Bali, very cheap, make you very happy. Aussie, Aussie, Aussie, yes?"

I'd have been very happy for Dodge to say, "Oi, Oi, Oi," and for us to keep walking, but that didn't happen.

"I don't want a gram, I want an ounce, how much?" Dodger asked, stepping forward into the smaller one's space.

I wasn't all that rattled that Dodger was yanking this bloke's chain, but I was unsure where the practical joke was going and how far Dodger would push it. Till we were arrested… or knifed?

"Special price, one ounce, maybe…" The kid pulled a calculator out of his pocket and punched in some numbers.

"Very good price, seven hundred Aussie dollar. You wait here. I get. Bring back, five minutes."

I was thinking he's pushed this as far as it's going to go. "Let's go Dodger, I need a cool drink."

He ignored me and continued to negotiate with the five-foot tall wheeler-dealer.

"Fuck off, five hundred."

"No, no, no. Seven hundred dollar. Very good price for Aussie Kangaroo."

With that, finally, Dodger turned and we both continued walking down the street.

The two locals were pissed that they had missed a pay day and followed us down the road, occasionally jumping in front of us to keep the conversation and haggling going.

"We talk to boss man, best price six hundred. Good? Good price? You come with me, free sample."

A hundred metres or so further on we found a bar that looked good enough and settled inside with a hundred other Australians in various stages of inebriation. Loud music and bad behaviour gave me the impression I was back in the Divers Tavern on a Friday night.

The drug dealers were turned away at the front door but stood out on the street for the next two hours waiting for us.

"Where were you taking that?" I asked, as I took the lid off my first Bintang.

"Curious what the going rate is up here. Your mate Pablo is charging us eight hundred and fifty an ounce on thirty-two ounces, right?"

"Yeah."

"Without trying, the street shit kickers are selling it for six hundred. If we found the supplier, we'd probably get it for three or four hundred an ounce. We'd kill a pig, Kat."

The twinkle in his eye and the enthusiasm in his voice suggested he had it all worked out.

"Okay, there are a couple of holes in your theory mate. Firstly, take the 'we' out. This is like my pearls. I do them, you can do this. There is no me up here. You're on your own in Bali, I'm not interested. You do know this is part of Indonesia, yeah? Secondly, who's looking after your quality control? Thirdly, how's it getting back to Broome? And, there's more, who do you reckon their boss is? Most likely the local police chief who will pocket your dough then arrest you for trafficking five minutes later. And then, Ole Mate, you'll be learning how to speak Indonesian while you see out your jail term. You ever seen their prisons? This ain't no TV in a single cell and games on Saturdays."

"Fine detail," he said laughing and I relaxed with the knowledge he'd just been trying it on… I hoped.

A lot later in the day, the dealers followed us back to the resort, tugging on Dodger's shirt every five steps, trying to negotiate a deal. But they were out of luck and were only given a two-word standard response.

We saw them both a few times over the next couple of days, always hanging around the front of the resort looking for business and homing in on Dodger every time he walked out the gate. A similar conversation took place each time, but the lead kid didn't move far off his original pricing scale.

Dodger finally tipped them over the edge when he poked the smaller one in the chest and told him he didn't need any speed because he had brought six ounces off 'your big friend at the tattoo place yesterday. Best price, very good quality' while waving a hand in the general direction of the main road.

Of course, there was no friend, no tattoo parlour and no dope. Dodge was just setting the bloke up and he took the hook.

Thinking he'd been done out of a payday that would have kept his family in luxury for a month, the drug dealer started screaming at Dodger in Indonesian, then he turned on his partner, pissed that he'd wasted time on us. The only part of his rant that I understood was the term, "Fucking Australians."

We walked away, joking that they must have hung around for three days waiting to lock down a deal and had been rolled by some non-existent tattoo parlour friend up town.

One of Dodger's tourist recommendations was a bus trip up to the active volcano at Ubud. We travelled the ninety minutes up to a small village in a twenty-seater bus with a variety of shaped and sized tourists from ten other countries.

After a bit of a tourist guide briefing and a legitimate fresh coconut milk drink from one that had its top chopped off in front of me, we were measured up on some reasonable quality 'Postie' type push bikes.

Instructed to roll down the mountain with the encouragement of, "No effort required. All downhill, use brakes, slowly, slowly." I set off behind Dodger.

Stopping at a couple of villages along the way, every local swamped the tourists, trying to flog off trinkets and sketches of the mountain. We weren't all that interested in the tourist crap, but we helped their economy by buying a couple of cold beers at each stopping point.

When we reached the tour end, where the bus was waiting, it was time to pay up. Dodger pulled out a credit card and I thought there was no way the guy would be able to take it, but he reached into a bag and pulled out a manual credit card imprint machine, just like the ones we had at home. He balanced it on his knee, held the paper copy in place with his elbow and laid Dodger's card on the platen. A couple of quick swipes with the roller over the top of the card and he handed the carbon imprint for Dodger to sign. Once done, we jumped on the bus.

"How much you had to drink?" I asked.

"Three beers, why?"

"How often do you pull that stunt?"

"What?"

"You just paid the bloke with your Medicare card!"

"Bullshit," he said, pulling out his wallet to have a look and the Medicare card was in the front row.

"Well, I'll be fucked. I didn't mean to do that. Honest." He grinned.

***

We decided to spend the afternoon at the resort and pulled up seats around the bar that sat out in the middle of the pool like an alcoholic island. The weather was hot and the atmosphere was most definitely holiday mode.

We'd just ordered our second beer when two reasonable looking Aussie tarts from a larger group of about eight or ten, swam up and plonked themselves either side of us. It wasn't rocket science to figure we were part of a bet between the birds as to who was going to pick up, 'the two blokes at the bar'.

Dodger bought the first round and pinned their ears back when he announced that if we were going to be drinking partners for the rest of the afternoon then half the bar tab was going on their room number. They looked quizzically at each other but must have decided we were worth the effort and agreed to the equality arrangement.

We had a ball all afternoon. The barman cranked up the music, we kept him on his toes with song requests, orders for a variety of food and copious amounts of alcohol. The two dolls were good value. Fun loving girls with a bit of character about them, they danced on the bar, sung and told as many dirty jokes as Dodger and I did. However, they made one big mistake. They tried to match us in the ability to absorb alcohol.

When day turned into night they started on champagne and the occasional Jägermeister chaser, a choice that Dodger and I wouldn't indulge in.

At some point, probably eight to ten hours into the session and noting that no one had left the submerged pool seats to go for a piss all day, the party got very ugly.

One of the birds had fallen asleep with her head on the bar but being that the rest of us were off our heads and uninterested in sleeping beauty, we didn't notice when she slid off the stool and disappeared under the water.

I'm a bit vague on the sequence of events that followed but there was shouting, yelling, people running everywhere, the barman came over the bar and jumped into the pool, there was chaos.

Person or persons unknown had seen what happened and dived in to stop our drinking partner from drowning. I remember seeing someone giving her CPR on the side of the pool and wondering how long the discipline of one hand on each breast had been CPR protocol. Last time I did the course it was one hand over the top of the other with pressure applied to the centre of the chest, not a gentle massage of each mammary gland.

Must have worked though as I also have a memory of her on all-fours spewing into a flower bed.

***

We had some difficulty leaving the country.

The resort's eight-seater dropped us off at Denpasar Airport and we wandered into the departure area with our half-empty soft sports bags over our shoulder. I noticed a few uniforms and guns sprinkled around the area, nothing unusual apart from the machine guns. You didn't see that in Australia. They might have been army, probably cops though. No big deal, just a passing interest from me in their choice of firearms.

As we stood in line to check in, a short-arse bloke wearing a shiny suit and with a lanyard around his neck, approached us. In perfect English, addressing us by our surnames, he said, "We are doing random bag checks today, would you mind following me please?"

The little prick caught me completely off guard and a million things jumped into my head. How does he know our names if it's a random check? Where are we going?

I realised I was praying. Please God, tell me Dodger didn't sneak out and do some fucking drug deal and has gear on him. Why are we surrounded by ten uniforms with machine gun barrels that were now at forty-five degrees? How the fuck is this going to unfold?

We were taken to a small office with a couple of tables in the centre. With ten to twelve blokes in the room, there wasn't room to swing a cat.

Standing behind one of the tables with his back to the wall was a guy who looked to me like a rooky cop, only because he didn't have a machine gun strapped over his shoulder. I noted that he had the holster strap of his handgun unclipped and his hand was resting on the butt of a gun. If there had been any gun protocols taught in the Indonesian Police Academy, this bloke was a no-show that day.

The original guy, Mr Shiny Suit was clearly in charge and barked orders in Indonesian to his subordinates. Our bags were dumped onto the tables and the contents of dirty jocks, smelly unwashed clothes and a couple of cheap and nasty T-shirts scattered about. The bags were tipped upside down and had the shit shaken out of them.

"Shirt and pants off," the main man ordered.

Dodger started to ark up. "Fuck off dickhead."

"Wheel it in Dodge, we're a bit outnumbered," I said, a lot more calmly than I felt.

We were told to stand in a star position while several hands ran over every wrinkle in our bodies. Under different circumstances, it wouldn't have been a bad experience.

Dodger had purchased a piece of timber wall art that you wouldn't have hung in your garden shed, but he thought it was going into his lounge room. The coppers hadn't been able to find a skerrick of anything of interest in our bags or strapped to our bodies so they decided there must have been contraband inside the woodwork and smashed it into a dozen pieces on the corner of the desk. All they got out of that was enough kindling to start a campfire.

With a little bow of the head from the boss cop, he said, "You are free to go, thank you for your cooperation."

Dodger pushed his luck. "Thank you. Where did you learn to speak English so well?"

"Kind of you to ask. I studied in the UK."

"Excellent," said Dodger. "Then you would be familiar with the expression, 'fuck you'?"

Silence.

Half the cops in the room knew enough English to get the drift of the conversation and flinched. The rooky with his hand still wrapped around his 9mm took a step forward.

Completely unfazed, the suit took a step closer, within arm's reach of Dodger. "It might be timely to remind you that your plane is due to depart in seventy minutes. If you would prefer to enjoy another week in Denpasar, albeit in custody, I would be pleased to assist you. If you were injured in the police van because you resisted arrest then you could be here for a couple of months."

After we checked-in and passed through customs we sat down to have a farewell coffee while waiting for our flight to be called.

"What's your take on all this?" Dodger asked, waving his hand in the direction of the four machine gun cops who had escorted us out of the search room and had shadowed us since.

"Well, it ain't rocket science, we were set up. My best guess is that your little mate out the front of the resort, that you wound up by telling him you'd brought a shit load off someone else, was connected to the cops somehow. The local police superintendent is probably the kid's principal supplier and he's lagged us in as having made a large purchase.

"Any cop could have rung the resort and found out our names, passport numbers, our return flight details and what resort bus to the airport we were going to be on. Or any variation of that."

"Makes sense," he agreed. "How else did the cop know our names anyway?"

"Don't know. You could have asked him if you hadn't told him to fuck off."

"Couldn't have anything to do with back home?" he asked.

"What, Broome? What do you mean?"

"Something has gone pear shaped back there, Aussie cops talk to Bali cops?"

"I doubt it, that's a big stretch. Someone would have rung us. You haven't spoken to anyone there, have you?" I asked with some concern.

"Only Tommy yesterday, he said fuck-all."

"Nah, I think it's something to do with the kid in the street. Anyway, we'll know in two hours when we get to Broome. If you see a couple of police cars on the tarmac, leg it."

The Hiding

Dodger had a habit of collecting people, some of them were good for all the right reasons, others were absolutely feral.

When the Dodger was still living in the caravan park, he had a shit head of a bloke living opposite. Unemployed, loudmouth, wife bashing, Mung Bean. They'd had a couple of run-ins over loud music and the usual shit you encounter with non-conformist individuals, but it came to a head when the clown backed his car into the corner of Dodger's caravan and then denied any knowledge of it.

Half-a-dozen other residents of the park who also hated the prick, saw it happen and lagged him into Dodger. They had a heated argument over the repair, but the bloke refused to admit or compensate.

Dodger reckons he was out-of-pocket five hundred bucks on the repair, so he had it in for the bloke. I'd been in the pub a couple of times when they had spotted each other and exchanged snarls. Dodger had baited the bloke with comments like, 'How's my five hundred going you fucking dog?' or 'I see your wife walked into the door again hey? Two black eyes this time, must be a fucking big door!' and shit like that.

Fair to say they weren't exactly on each other's Christmas card lists.

We had had a relatively early Friday knock off and had arranged to have two beers at the front bar of a pub in China Town. Don't ask me why we decided that was a good idea. It was the roughest pub in Broome, same venue where Pablo had shown me how the real world of illicit drugs worked. The bar furniture was still the Kimberley classic, concrete and bolted down. You wouldn't have taken your mother-in-law there unless you'd wanted her out of your life. Maybe it was because we were still in stinking, sweaty work shorts and T-shirts with the sleeves cut out. Perhaps we thought we'd blend in well. Whatever the reason, it was dumb.

I had dropped the Pom off at the hospital for her afternoon shift and had arrived at the bar five minutes before Dodger. He had been in the next street dropping off a shit load of white and green to Bill and Ben.

We considered ourselves cleanskins for the weekend again, the factory office was closed and the drug supply orders were filled. Business was declared closed for the week, beer o'clock it was.

The bar was half full and quite rowdy for so early in the afternoon. The two of us were sitting on high stools over a high table and into our second beer when I spotted Caravanman walking up behind Dodger preparing to poor a beer over his head.

He had two other fuckers flanking him.

Before I had time to warn Dodger, I was king hit on the side of the face and spun off my chair. I didn't go down, but I did see stars for a second and a cut opened along my cheekbone. I launched myself back at the shit head that had hit me and we traded half-a-dozen blows before it quickly turned into a wrestle and both of us fell to the floor.

When confronted with this sort of event your adrenaline skyrockets in an instant and it comes down to instinct; survive and kill the opposition. You'll fight like you're the third monkey on Noah's Ark and it's just started to rain.

If you get the upper hand, the last thing you are going to do is let the bloke get up if he hasn't been hurt. If he does, he'll usually get up twice as angry as he was before and that might not work in your favour.

I had this fucker in a headlock and started dragging his head over the 12mm dyna bolts anchoring the table. I can remember the crunching sound of his forehead making contact.

Someone dragged me off him and I was flung under another table. I curled up against the steel legs trying to protect my head while some pricks who weren't wearing thongs, sank the boots in.

It was a decent flogging, with more than one boot making contact at any given time. I'd cop a kick in the back of the head and pull my hands up over then I'd get a boot in the back and try to protect my inner organs, then another wack in the head, always too late for the hit. Not sure the arseholes had it choreographed like that but that's how it unfolded. I had no choice but to ride it out.

The bouncers arrived and sorted out a few others that had jumped into the fight, or started their own, just because it was Friday at this shit hole and that's what you did.

What I hadn't seen, because I was a bit busy saving my own life, was that before Caravanman had finished pouring the beer over Dodger's head, Dodge had spun around and landed a perfect straight right to the nose that dropped the dipstick, cold as a spud on the concrete floor.

Now as handy as the Dodger was, two on one didn't work real well and the other two ring-ins got stuck into him.

I never figured out if we had been set up or if it was just a spur of the moment decision by Caravanman to settle a score while he had some soldiers with him and was motivated by liquid courage. However, it did seem odd that the only ones wearing steel capped boots in the bar that day were the blokes kicking the shit out of us.

I rolled over on my back and stayed put for a while, mainly because I couldn't breathe. I saw Dodger on all-fours spitting blood on the floor and Caravanman was still having a sleep.

A young Aboriginal kid we had working for us, Kevin, had been sitting a couple of tables behind us and had witnessed the whole shit fight. I'm pleased he didn't get involved as he was a lightweight kid and would have got hurt.

He could see Dodge and I were both knocked around, blood pissing out everywhere, both of us having trouble to walk or talk.

The kid played the game exceptionally well and with a couple of his mates, helped us to our feet, managed us out the door and rolled both of us into the back of his ute. He drove us straight around to the hospital emergency door and helped us get inside.

Dodger's head looked like it had been on fire and someone had put it out with a cricket bat. He was probably thinking the same thing about me.

Being that it was late afternoon there weren't a lot of people in the emergency department waiting to be attended to. Another eight or ten hours later on a Friday night, when serious alcohol took hold and the queue would have been halfway down the street. I could smell a strange mix of alcohol tinged with disinfectant and a side whiff of urine. I almost gagged.

We sat ourselves down in the middle of a row of thirty-year-old plastic chairs. The other fifteen or so patients sprinkled around the waiting room represented the community of Broome from one end of the spectrum to the other. A grey nomad sat in front of me with a towel wrapped around his hand. According to the story he told the nurse who had come to look at him, the tops of two fingers were missing courtesy of his caravan jack slipping. An old indigenous lady with her 12-year-old granddaughter standing at her side, was having serious difficulties breathing. No idea what the ailment was but I quietly hoped she saw a doctor real soon or the kid would be leaving by herself. A local indigenous man, reeking of drink and who I had seen many a time sitting in the middle of the Kennedy Hill wasteland, was slumped over two chairs. While he may have been waiting for a kidney dialysis machine to become available, I imagined the first priority would have been to adjust his blood-alcohol level. A couple of seats up from Dodger, sat an immaculately dressed woman in her sixties, with more gold on her fingers than the Kalgoorlie super pit. From what I could see, she had broken a fingernail. Although who knew. She could have been riddled with VD. No telling just on appearances.

After a while a nurse came over and took down some briefing notes to ascertain our triage status and a couple of minutes later the Pom, who was working in the ED office, came out and stepped into both of us big time.

There is an expectation that nurses, and hospital staff in general, are calm and caring in the execution of their duties, but not this one. She was ropable that we would turn up at her place of employment in this condition and assumed that it had all been of our own making. Standing in front of us with her hands on her hips, she delivered a magnificent spray, worthy of any grand final footy coach.

And she was relentless.

Stuff like, "When are you two fucking Muppets going to grow up?"

"Are you serious coming in here like this?"

"You have embarrassed me, you idiots."

And on and on… and on it went.

At this stage her own personal, and family, history had to be factored in. Her grandfather had been a runner for the Kray twins in the East End of London. The fruit didn't fall far from the tree and the Pom's father had continued the family tradition of earning an income from armed robberies, protection rackets, arson and assaults.

By the time the Pom had reached her teenage years she had witnessed a ridiculous amount of skulduggery and assaults, including savage domestic violence episodes directed on an aunt that shook her to the core.

She made a commitment to herself to move her own life in a different direction. She didn't want a career as a crook and she was never going to allow anyone to force her into the corner of a room for the purpose of having the shit belted out of her.

She joined a local Aikido dojo as 'Plan A', with the intention of being confident enough to defend herself if it was ever required. Quickly developing a passion for the art and thriving on the exercise and self-discipline required, she moved to Maastricht in the Netherlands for nine months to train under a world-respected Master. By the time she returned to London she was a 3rd Kyu, two grades off Black Belt.

On returning to London a part-time boyfriend took offence to her telling him he needn't bother coming around again. In a drunken rage he'd sat her on her arse and given her a couple of solid clouts to the head. In due course her father sorted the ex-boyfriend out, it cost the bloke a fortune to have his broken teeth repaired, but it was a reality check, a decisive moment for the Pom.

She was a very experienced and competent martial arts student who could competently defend herself in the sterile environment of a padded classroom, but that wasn't the real world. She wanted to learn how to give a bit back the other way.

As was the case with the East End gangsters, stretching out over generations, most were connected to gyms and the boxing game. It wasn't acceptable for a female to be seen in a ring unless she was the dolly bird wearing a bikini and holding the round numbers up, but the Pom's old man had an associate in his back pocket who owed him a few favours. She was introduced to an ex-WW2 veteran of Burmese decent who was a Master in, 'Bando Thaing'. It's a cross discipline of traditional boxing and kick boxing. Four times a week, one on one with a Master of the trade, when no one else was in the building, the Pom developed the skills to attack as well as defend.

I'd had a few fun spars with her around the house, but we were only fooling and she never seriously tried to take my head off. She told me the only 'real blue' she'd been in was when her half-brother took a swing at her and she broke his nose.

Over a beer in the backyard one day, she and Dodger were sharing war stories when she jumped up and declared, "Come on big boy, I'll take you on."

With that the two of them danced around like Muhammad Ali and traded soft blows for five minutes while I watched on in awe.

Dodger would tell me later, "You're a run-of-the-mill street brawler Kat, you're not worth a cold pie. The Pom is the real deal, she's been trained properly, she's a fighter.

"She reads and registers a hit with thought, guidance and accuracy. It comes with experience and training. And I'll give you a little tip, watch her feet. Most of her moves are defensive, that's how she was taught through Aikido, but use your peripheral vision and watch the position of her feet. If she stands up on her toes like a fucking kangaroo, she's swapped from defence to offence and you're about to have a roundhouse kick delivered to your throat or front teeth."

This last comment was well and truly in the front of our minds while we both pushed our backs hard into the vinyl chairs in ED and focused on the position of her feet.

She only weighed in around sixty kilos but was threatening like a human windmill about to unleash. Neither of us said a word, we were both shit scared she'd start throwing punches or a roundhouse in our direction and then we would have been fucked.

Not once did she ask, 'what happened?' or 'are you okay?'

After a while she calmed down enough to have us admitted by other staff but she'd made it perfectly clear she didn't want anything to do with us.

Dodger said to me, "I was waiting for you to tell her to shut the fuck up."

"Yeah, you're a hero too. I didn't see your mouth move."

A couple of hours later we had been cleaned up, X-rays taken and some stitches put in under my eye where the first hit got me. The cut perfectly matched my rimless sunglasses so when anyone asked me later what happened I just told them I'd walked into a door with my glasses on. It was a more acceptable story than admitting to a belting at the pub.

Dodger still looked like a lion had chewed on his head, lumps, bumps and welts all over him, but both of us were relieved that nothing appeared to be broken.

We were given the okay to leave, so I asked the Pom if she would like me to come back and pick her up at the end of her shift. She still had the shits on and didn't lift her head to offer up the surly reply of, "Don't bother."

We shuffled out of the emergency department, past the Kennedy Hill drunk who was by then on the floor snoring his guts out, surrounded by a circle of piss. The journey back to my place was very slow, staggering, holding our ribs and our kidneys in position as we shuffled along.

As we approached my place we could see both our vehicles parked up, noses of the cars against the front verandah.

"Good kid that one, hey?" said Dodger.

"Kevin? Yeah, good value."

After Kevin had dropped us off at ED, he'd recruited his mates to get both our vehicles back from China Town to my place. The minor detail that none of them held a motor vehicle driver's licence didn't seem to be a sticking point. I slung him fifty bucks when I caught up with him a couple of days later for putting his hand up when we needed him.

He had been lacking a bit of family structure but came across as a talented kid who was happy to work and improve on his disadvantaged upbringing. He had learnt how to weld and read a tape measure through TAFE and we were more than happy with him working for us.

Dodger and I went and watched him play football a few times as a show of support. He had terrific ball skills like a lot of the kids have in the top end.

Sadly he had to pack the job in when he had two very young kids dumped on him, 'to look after'. He was sixteen.

Four years later he served some jail time for pointing a loaded .22 calibre rifle at the chests of two coppers in a Broome laneway. It was only the professionalism of the cops that avoided anyone dying in the pindan that day.

When we got back into my joint, we settled into some amber pain killers, sitting outside in the warm night air and discussing our luck at not being in ICU.

Dodger's wife, who had returned from Adelaide the week before, turned up to take him home, but she had arrived with an attitude that didn't quite align with Dodger's. The sour, eye-piercing stare she offered suggested that her opinion of me hadn't improved while she'd been away. By the time they got to my front door they were giving each other a decent mouthful and I clearly heard him tell her it was time she fucked off permanently. "Feel free to move out anytime you want. I'll help you pack."

She made a full-blown attempt to slam the front flywire door off its hinges on the way out. In response, he grabbed two more beers from the fridge and returned outside with me.

The Pom walked in a short time later, still dressed in nurses' attire. She kicked her shoes off and pulled a beer of her own out of the fridge, sitting down at the end of the table glaring at us both.

I was really hoping she wasn't going to start up again. After listening to Dodger and his wife ark up I'd regained enough courage to contemplate telling her to pull her head in if she did.

The stare slowly eased, the scowl twisted into a smile, she took a swig and nearly choked. The laughing came between gasps and spluttering and turned into hysterics. The Dodge and I looked at each other, sensed the atmospheric change and given the sight of her rolling around choking on half a mouthful of beer we joined in with her laughing.

When she had her composure back, in her best Pommy accent she muttered, "You dickheads."

It was the ice breaker. We were mates again.

"You will be pleased to note that your medical files have been marked up as, 'Wombat'."

"Doesn't sound like a medical term to me. You know in Australian slang that calling a person a Wombat is slightly derogative? Because what does a Wombat do? It eats, roots and leaves. Get it?" I asked her.

"Yes, I know that one. It was one of the first things I learnt when I arrived in Australia. I'm talking about the medical term, 'Wombat with a silent F'."

"Wombat doesn't have an F in it."

She was struggling to keep a straight face and I sensed she was taking the piss.

"It does when it refers to you two. Waste Of Fucking Money, Breath And Time. Wombat." And she roared with laughter, spending the next five minutes cackling and giggling her tits off at her own stupid joke. A few times she got close to getting her act together but cracked up again. When she could finally put a sentence together, she told us that two others had presented at ED during her shift, courtesy of the punch up at the pub. One, who we figured was the Caravanman, would be sent by flying doctor back to Perth the next day to have his broken nose and cheekbone operated on. The other patient required multiple stitches to lacerations across his forehead.

Dodger wanted to burn the Caravanman's residence down that night, but I talked him out of it. It might have been a bit obvious.

The Caravanman disappeared about a week later. The prick had left town.

***

About a month after the punch up we decided to have a quiet Sunday afternoon at home. It was the last round of the AFL regular season and the Eagles were playing Footscray late in the arvo. Dodger had the big-breasted dolly bird from the Divers Tavern in tow and the Pom was rostered off for the day. We had a couple of rounds of drinks and just before half time, it was a shit game, Dodger and I jumped in one of the utes to pick up some Chinese takeaway in town.

We pulled up in front of the restaurant and parked beside a late-model dual cab in good nick. We'd had to stand aside to let a bloke carrying two bags of food out the front door. The bloke looked at me, I looked at him and I was thinking, 'how do I know you?', then I saw the healing scars on his forehead. He was a little thinner and younger than I'd remembered him.

"Hey, shit for brains," I called out. Dodger had no idea what was going on and jumped in real quick. "What?"

"Caravanman's mate," I replied as the bloke put his two full bags of takeaway on the bonnet of the flash dual cab and spun around.

"You got no mates here today hey?" I asked.

Dodger had twigged to who the bloke was and we both stepped forward, the adrenaline kicking in.

It only took a fraction of a second for the bloke to decide his health would be better if he left. He spun on one foot and took off faster than either of us could have matched. By the time he'd run ten metres or so into the street he was in serious flight mode. Not once did he look back before he crossed over into China Town, avoided a couple of cars and disappeared out of sight.

Dodger was fired up at seeing the prick and proceeded to kick both wing mirrors off the ute, so they hung down by the electrical wires. Then he bent the wipers back far past their usual position. I grabbed the tucker off the bonnet, both plastic bags were full, twice what our order was going to be.

"Enough food here for half the street, Dodge. That'll do us hey?"

The Bottom Feeders

I was suffering a moral ambiguity about being a drug dealer.

Of course the Dodger and I did not see the title applied to us. We regarded ourselves as financial mercenaries. Mind you, both activities are illegal in Australia.

What we saw was a business opportunity. A simplistic business model of the supply and demand of a product. We purchased at a wholesale price and resold at a marked-up value. Having sourced a wholesale supplier of goods we found customers who were willing to purchase those same goods at an eye-watering minimum one-hundred percent price increase. And they paid cash up front. The ATO and the Child Support Agency wouldn't see a cent.

The greatest advantage we had was that neither of us were users. I admit to having dipped a finger into the white powder as a taste test on half-a-dozen occasions but that was the extent of my usage. Pablo's advice not to do that was well noted and he had been correct, it did taste like shit and it did have me bouncing off the walls. Dodger probably knocked off a bud of Gunja now and again but that didn't classify him as a raging drug addict either.

So our uncomplicated interest was purely a financial one.

Amphetamine, AKA Go, Goey, Clout, Whippa, Hit, Up, Amp, Speed, White, was not a new drug on the scene, it was first invented in Germany in 1887. It took a while to get off the ground but by the 1930's was being produced as a 'Decongestant'.

During World War II most armies used it at one time or another to 'increase alertness and give added physical strength'.

In the 1970's the United Nations declared it a Schedule II controlled substance but in Australia, in the early to mid-80's, it could still be purchased legally over the counter in the form of Ephedrine.

After that it rapidly became the illegal drug of choice, outstripping heroin and had been manufactured in clandestine drug labs since. With the increase of illegal use, and the community disruption that caused, came the crack down on the policing of its use and manufacturing of the substance.

Fines, imprisonment, seizure of property and assets steadily increased over the years to reflect the seriousness of the problem, but in the early 90's the game was only just starting.

One question we often asked ourselves but consciously never asked our customers was where all this dope was going? Some offered the information up in general conversation but there was no obligation to bring us into the loop. It was just curiosity on our behalf as to who in their right mind would pay a hundred and twenty dollars for a gram of white powder that made you feel like you were King Kong for twelve hours?

These people were the "Bottom Feeders". The end of the food chain, the last person to be standing in the line after the product had been passed down through several hands from the point of manufacture to the end user.

Not all bottom feeders are drug addicts and I'd never met anyone who admitted to being one anyway, but a large percentage are. There would be individuals who might lash out once a month, some once a week. A genuine bottom feeder was banging it in daily.

And for this lunatic, I have no sympathy whatsoever.

Whether this individual was born with the gene that inhibits their ability to comprehend right from wrong, good from bad, enough is enough, or they were born with foetal alcohol syndrome, or they suffered a head injury falling out of their highchair, is all arguable. In my opinion what they collectively have is weakness of character.

Addiction comes in many forms. It can be the person who requires the muscle burn of pumping weights in the gym every day, it might be the bike rider who craves the wind in his face or the office secretary who must have her double-espresso almond milk on the way to the office.

The big difference between these individuals and the bottom feeders is that these people have the ability and strength of character to adjust or alter their addiction to suit their lifestyles without damaging relationships, blowing their Centrelink payments or stealing an old lady's handbag from the supermarket trolley.

The gym is closed because it's a public holiday, so the gym junkie takes his or her dog for a walk around the block.

The bike rider cannot ride to work because it's pissing rain, he catches the train.

Run out of almond milk, soy will be fine.

The bottom feeder has had a thousand opportunities to make corrections to his lifestyle on his ride down the slippery slope, but he's ignored every one of them.

He is weak.

He does not have the ability to think ahead to what his obligations or commitments are tomorrow or in a week's time. He is a rudderless human being, an insipid, thieving, lying, deceitful individual.

He has developed a cognitive impairment that punishes and tortures anyone and everyone who crosses his path.

Or hers of course. This is an equal-opportunities affliction.

This person is not your friend. They do not give a rat's arse about you or what's going on in your life.

If you are unfortunate enough to have the need to talk to one of these fleabags, you will note that one of their most obvious traits is that everything that happens with their life is someone else's fault.

They are completely incapable of accepting that any decision in their miserable life was their fault. Regardless of the subject, someone else did it or is to blame.

The car ran out of fuel.

The prick that borrowed it two weeks ago didn't put fuel in it.

Can't turn up to work more than two days in a row.

Grandmother's sick, dog ran away.

Got knocked off for driving a stolen car.

Blame the coppers for pulling me over.

Their greatest con is convincing their doctor and their family that they have been living with the medical condition known as Bipolar. In their mind it justifies their erratic behaviour. They don't have Bipolar, they have a fucking drug addiction.

But by claiming that Bipolar is the problem they then have access to a ridiculous amount of dangerous prescription drugs that they can legally throw in on top of their amphetamine and Gunja use which remains the underlying problem. So the problem escalates and is compounded by the cocktail of mood stabilisers, antipsychotic, antidepressant, anti-anxiety drugs and half-a-dozen joints a day that the dickhead has convinced himself is necessary to treat a mental disorder that he does not have.

He (or she) gets injured, scrapes a knee or breaks a fingernail and the next challenge is to convince the ED doctor that they have an extremely low-pain threshold and cannot leave the hospital without a script for enough pain killing Opioid medication to kill a black dog. Their doctor shopping routine is now amped up to include their reliance on Hillbilly heroin.

At some stage they finish in a courtroom where their legal-aid solicitor attempts to treat the magistrate like a moron, claiming that their client seeks leniency due to their poor family upbringing, (part of the blaming everyone else process) and their mental health issues that they don't have.

The solicitor will deliver a rousing speech explaining that his client is very understanding of the predicament that he now finds himself in and is genuinely seeking access to drug and alcohol rehabilitation programs.

Meanwhile, the druggie who is standing beside the solicitor is fidgeting so badly it's sending everyone else in the courtroom nuts and he is looking around the room trying to see who the solicitor is talking about because it sure as fuck isn't him. More chance of him flying to the moon than fronting up to a rehab clinic.

His concentration is focused on the concealed snap lock bag rolled up in his underpants and when he can pull it out rather than play with the package through the lining of his pocket.

What the solicitor fails to tell the court is that the mental health issue is a bi-product of being a raging, out of control, useless fucking drug addict incapable of helping himself or being helped by any well-intended agency or individual either.

The greatest loser in this human shit fight is the immediate family, predominantly the parents. Those that love him and care for him the most. They first start to feel disenfranchised when accused of not offering love or softness. When they start asking hard questions of their child they will be fobbed off with comments like, 'I'm too stressed to talk about that right now'.

The mood swings will intensify and everyone under the same roof will be forced to walk around on eggshells, shit scared to utter a word in case it starts a blue.

The caring parents will travel a long way with him on his journey, holding their hand out, offering help and guidance. At every opportunity they will plead with him to make changes and become a good person again. They will do their best to explain that pure pleasure in life doesn't have to be expensive or addictive, there is a wholesome life beyond drug abuse.

The druggie nods his head and smiles, telling the family what they want to hear, not necessarily anything that resembles the truth or fact.

The family bubble eventually bursts when things start disappearing from the house and dad's expensive Nikon camera finishes up at a pawn shop.

They eventually cut their losses and walk away in tears.

As the druggie wanders off into the sunset, screaming his guts out and punching holes in the wall he will be cursing his family. It's all their fault. None of it is the individual's fault. None of it.

Did anyone ever progress from a non-drug user to a hopeless addict because they started on amphetamines that passed through our hands?

I don't know.

But what if they did?

Was it forced upon them? Whose decision was it to hand over the hundred or hundred and twenty bucks for their first clout? Whose decision was it to have another crack at it a week later? Who thought it was a good idea to rip a hunge out of grandma's purse or steal the neighbour's new television set?

Not us.

I only supplied a need.

If not me then someone else.

It wasn't my fa—

Enforcing the Law

Tommy was having problems with a couple of kids that had moved into the house opposite him. Thirteen and fourteen-year old's that were clearly not engaged in school activities and were hanging out in the street playing shit heads all day.

Since they had moved in there had been eight house break-ins in the street, half the cars had been damaged or ransacked and spray paint graffiti was all over the place.

Tommy's wife had caught them on her verandah twice and she was a bit fragile about her security which had Tommy on the back foot. He was getting too old to be challenging the kids and asked us how we would handle the situation.

The father of the kids was having a go in life and had a full-time job with the shire. He must have been a reliable, long-term employee as he had access to a shire ute that was parked up on the property after hours. The mother was nowhere to be seen so the kids were running riot while the old man was at work all day.

Dodger jumped into the conversation and offered to, 'sort it out'.

"You can't use my name," pleaded Tommy.

"You won't get a mention Tommy. Trust me."

Dodger pulled his ute into the drive and parked behind the shire vehicle. The two shit heads were sitting on the verandah of an old timber-clad house that would have been the first one ever built in the street. The place was scruffy and overgrown with trees that probably helped keep the house cool with the amount of shade covering it.

"Your dad home?"

"Who the fuck wants ta' know?" asked the smart-arse elder one.

"Wrong answer kid," replied Dodger, who proceeded to pull out a four-litre can of fuel from the back of his ute.

He walked past the kids and knocked loudly on the front door. The kids went a bit gun shy and legged it around to the back of the house. There was a bit of crashing and banging going on inside and eventually the dad opened the flywire door.

A hard looking fellow who looked like he was under some life-pressures stood there, still wearing his shire uniform. He didn't appear to be all that pleased with having been pulled away from his couch and afternoon beer, watching the GWN repeat of 'Hogan's Heroes' on the TV.

"Hi," said Dodger, pulling on his caring professional persona. "Sorry to interrupt. Mr Wymond isn't it?"

Dodger had asked a couple of blokes he knew at the shire depot what the bloke's name was and any history, good or bad, that he should be aware of. Nothing he heard had frightened him off.

"I live just down the street a bit and a few of the neighbours have asked me to have a quiet chat with you about your boys."

"What now?" The bloke replied, with a bit of attitude in his voice.

"They going to school?"

"Supposed to be."

"Well, that might be the problem, they're not. They're in the street all day tormenting the neighbourhood." Dodger had changed his tone from placid to dangerous.

"It's a bit hard, I'm working full-time and I can't keep them under control when I'm not here." The guy offered up in a dismissive tone.

Dodger bent over and unscrewed the cap off the petrol can so they could both smell the fumes.

"Hey, stop. Fuck, what you doing man?"

There was now panic as the guy sensed a shit fight in the making.

"How long would it take for you to find accommodation if you couldn't live here?" asked Dodger.

"No, no. Please. Come on man, what are you doing? I waited two years to get this place. Please, don't. No trouble, please."

"That's exactly what's going to happen. No more trouble. To-morrow the kids go back to school and they will be there every day. Not one foot out of line, no more graffiti, house break-in's, car break-in's, no abusing or swearing at people in the street. Are we on the same page here? Or will the three of you be living in the back of your Broome Shire ute?"

"Yes, yes. Please leave. No more problems, I promise."

"Then let's be very fucking clear." Dodger had raised his voice and poked the dad in the chest for emphasis. "That's the rules and they start right now. You going to speak to your boys, or you want me too? You all need to take me very fucking seriously because if I have to come back again it'll be three o'clock in the morning and you won't see me coming."

"I'll fix it man. Please. Fuck man, please. Take the petrol away. No trouble please."

A month later Dodger asked Tommy how his neighbours were going?

"They walk out of the house in the morning and back into the house after school. They haven't been seen in the street since you went around there. What did you say to them?"

"Not much. Just encouraged the father to engage a bit better with them."

***

Dodger and I were sharing a ride home together from a shire meeting and drove past our factory on the way. It wasn't late, maybe 10:00 pm and we'd only had one beer in us, so it hadn't been a big night in any way.

As we drove past our factory, we could see four or five shadows scurrying around the inside of the fence line like fucking cockroaches. We pulled up two driveways down, parked up and snuck back along the chain link fence, half hidden by the blooming pink bougainvillea growing on it. As we got closer, we could hear the fuckers trying to kick the PA door in. Dodger very gently unlocked the front gate and we tried to sneak up behind them but the gravel under our polished leather dress shoes gave us away.

They took off in four different directions. The best I could manage was a torn smelly T-shirt and a hand full of black hair. Dodger cornered one of them down the side of the factory, a kid about fourteen years old. He had him on the ground sinking polished leather into him, trying out some Fred Astaire footwork up and down the kids' body when I arrived.

"Okay, okay. Don't kill him here," I said, trying to back Dodger off a bit.

We had a fairly common game we would play with people when we were both in the mood and having a joke. We read each other well, role-playing bullshit when we wanted and pulled it on with this kid.

"What are we going to do with him?" asked Dodger.

"We don't have a choice. We have to kill him."

The kid was rolling around the pindan and wasn't happy. Dodger had given him enough to slow him down and he was sulking a bit in the process. So, we stood over the top of him discussing his fate.

"I'm not digging the fucking hole. I did it last time and the ground was that hard it took me two hours to bury the bloke."

The kid was taking all this in and started pissing in his pants. It was highly unlikely that a kid whose family didn't give a shit where he was at night would be unfamiliar with copping a belting, but being caught and having two blokes stand over the top of him planning his death was different. It un-nerved him a touch.

"Make him dig the hole," said Dodger.

"Yeah, good idea. I'll grab a shovel out of the ute and he can start digging right here. When it's deep enough, we take his head off with the shovel and fill the hole in. If we pull that pot plant over the hole, no one will ever know. But this time, I'll hit him in the head with the shovel. Last time you did it, it took you four hits before the bloke died. The first hit needs to be here." And I tapped the back of his head with the toe of my shoe.

The shit head had rolled over on his side and had started to cry, whispering, "No, no."

"Don't take it too personal son, we just have to stop you shit heads breaking into other people's property and the best way to stop it happening is to bury you. What's your name anyway?"

He whimpered out his name and I pretended to write it on the back of my hand.

"And your mates, what's their names?"

He hesitated. "I can't tell you, they'll kill me."

"It won't matter, you'll be dead and under that pot plant in half an hour anyway. What's their names?"

Between sobs, he offered up another three names.

"When we find them, we'll bury them beside you. You okay with that?"

He didn't answer.

"I'll grab the shovel. You get some rope so we can tie his hands behind his back so we can take his head off."

"Don't move kid, I don't want to have to chase you and get more blood on my best shoes," offered up Dodger with a wink and we both took a couple of steps back.

As anticipated, the kid took off at a thousand miles an hour, albeit with a limp from the corked thighs Dodger had given him with his size 11's.

Dodger cupped his hands to his mouth but made no effort to move. At the top of his voice he yelled, "Get him, get him! Kill him, kill him."

The only effect it had on the kid was that his stride lengthened.

He disappeared out through the front gate, last seen heading towards Port Drive.

We both laughed our guts out.

"How long before they're back?" asked Dodger.

"I'll give it two months."

Prison Games

I drove into the yard one day to see Dodger standing beside a new prison transfer van and chatting to a couple of blokes in uniform.

When he walked back inside I said to him, "Bit premature, we haven't been caught yet."

"Just building up some brownie points for us both, just in case."

"That's very thoughtful of you. And what did they really want?"

"We've done a deal. Once again, we will be seen as the honourable, community-spirited businesspeople you keep telling me we are."

He was having a dig at me. "This will be good coming from you, go on."

"They wanted to know if we would take on a couple of indigenous blokes, on a part-time basis. It's to do with their pre-release requirements. Three hours, twice a week, nine till midday. They drop them off, they pick 'em up. There's a government subsidy, forty bucks a day for taking them on."

"And?" I enquired.

"They start next Tuesday."

This was one small step for man and one giant leap for The Dodger.

The man never ceased to amaze me. As hard and cold as he could be and knowing his previous history where conflict had been involved, this was a big leap forward for him to draw a line in the sand and offer someone not as privileged as himself a hand up.

He'd done the deal and he was proud of it. I nodded my head in agreement.

The Broome Prison had a reputation around town as being a bit laid-back, even by Kimberley standards. There had been rumours going around for ages about inmates jumping the fence at night-time, walking up to Kennedy Hill and getting on the grog. Before daybreak they'd jump the back fence and wander back to their cells.

I'm not sure that everyone in town believed the story but it ballooned into reality when the cohorts got so drunk one night they couldn't scale the fence to get back in. They were found sound asleep, drunk as monkeys, on the outside of the perimeter fence.

Our two inmates were dutifully dropped off a few days later and we had already discussed giving them meaningful jobs. We had quite a few steel beams that needed to be wirer brushed and given a coat of paint. The beams were set up on trestles in the lean-to, out of the sun. We pre-mixed the paint and plugged the spray gun into the compressor.

I'm a born and bred Australian who has an acceptable understanding of indigenous culture. However, I confess to only being able to speak about five words of the local Broome dialect. This from a language history that has hundreds of different variants, let alone dialects, across the whole of Australia. It all adds up to potential communication problems.

So these two guys turn up and they are clearly from an extremely remote part of the Kimberley. They appeared clean and tidy and were extremely friendly with big broad smiles and plenty of facial hair, but I had absolutely no idea what they were saying. Even when I thought they understood English, or my version of it, they were talking back to me in a tongue that had no connection to my brain.

Not one word did I understand and I had not the slightest clue if they understood anything I said other than them nodding.

The first day went off tremendously well. I showed them what to do, they got the drift and were good at it. I bought them a pie and soft drink each off the smoko truck and everyone got on fabulously.

The screws picked them up at lunch time and we all swapped smiles and waved.

Day two started well but didn't finish so good.

We were doing okay up to the point where I brought them another round of meat pies and a change in their diet to choc milks. I left the food on the smoko table as everyone gathered around but got called away to the office. Ten minutes later I came back out. The inmates were nowhere to be seen, the pies were still in the paper bags on the table.

"Where's our two labourers?" I asked.

No one had seen them, so I went for a walk.

Down the back of the factory, on the inside of the building, was a small garden shed where we kept our flammable consumables, paint, thinners and small quantities of fuel. I found the two guys sitting on the floor of the shed with their heads hanging over open four-litre cans of paint between their legs. They were completely motherless, off their heads on the fumes.

Dodger was devastated that his nomination for 'Citizen of the Year' would have to wait.

Close Calls

Despite not being nominated for 'Citizen of the Year', we were making upwardly mobile movements. If we needed proof, then we got it when we received an invitation from a local Rotary Club official to enter a team in the annual Dragon Boat Regatta.

Being that we both had some athletic/physical fitness history in our lives, albeit a long time ago, we embraced the idea. The team was entered under the business name and we recruited the bodies we needed from employees, wives, girlfriends and a couple of clients. The team of eighteen were required to be half fit, a hundred percent keen, be capable of drinking beer between events and swim. Women crew members were encouraged to wear bikinis to distract other competitors.

A couple of weeks before the event we borrowed one of the Dragon boats that was stored in a shed on Port Drive and took it down to Town Beach for a training run. Our mob were hopeless and that was before we pulled the esky out. After they had fallen out of the boat a few times and rowed around in circles, Dodger pulled them all in for a pep talk.

There was a fair bit of Broome pride riding on this, kudos and bragging rights for twelve months and we were determined to win it. Dodger gave a rousing speech with a plea that concentrating for two minutes would be really helpful.

The technique required to power the boat wasn't rocket science. Using his firsthand knowledge of the rowing discipline, he instructed them all to call out the word, 'stroke' in unison and make sure that their oar hit the water at the same time as everyone else's. Stroke… stroke… stroke.

We balanced out the boat so it wasn't lopsided. Heavy weights on either side, a dolly bird falling out of a white bikini up the front, banging the drum, pretending she knew what she was doing and joining in with the chant, me down the back steering.

By the end of the training session everyone believed they were on the Olympic team.

Race day was full of spectacular Broome weather, turquoise blue water, live music, food tents, laughter and a few cool drinks.

And our work-sponsored team won the day.

A fair bit later in the arvo, Dodger and I were walking back to his ute parked up on Robinson Street. Carrying a very large, mostly empty, esky between us we turned the corner and were met by every police car in Broome with its lights flashing. An RBT. Everyone leaving Town Beach was getting knocked off.

It would be fair to say that the two of us would have given .05 a big nudge which was the first problem. As we walked up to the front of the queue we saw Dodger's ute, parked inside the cordoned off area, directly behind the booze bus. A couple of coppers using it as a leaning post. Dodger steered me and the esky away from the action with a soft, "Just keep walking."

So we did, up to the beer garden of the Conti Hotel.

"Putting aside the drunk driving charge we just avoided, what's in the ute?" I enquired.

"Not much."

He was stalling, I could tell.

"Half a pound and a few bucks under the font seat."

He was still being evasive. "How many bucks?" I asked.

"Fifteen grand, give or take a bit." He replied with a sheepish grin.

"Jesus Christ." I was a bit taken aback by his admission that the ute was loaded up. We had been operating under a fairly good system where dope and dough would only be in our possession for the absolutely minimum of time, sometimes only minutes, an hour at the most. This wasn't how we had agreed to run the show.

"I knew today would be a circus and Bill & Ben want a top up tonight. I thought it might save me a head fuck later."

"I'll share a little newsflash with you mate," I said, anger beginning to bubble up. "If either of us had put the keys in the ignition, we'd be walking or riding bikes for the next six months. If they decided to have a look in the ute at the same time, the only walking we'd be doing would be laps around the prison oval.

"Having two coppers resting their arse against the ute, half a meter away from fifteen large and another eight in white is a head fuck."

He looked at me with a grin. "Yeah. So… We having another beer?"

My anger popped like a balloon. "Might as well, we're not going back to the car for a while."

***

A few weeks after the regatta I'd driven the old, flat-tray Toyota we owned around to the freight depot to pick up the Pablo fridge that I was confident had arrived overnight.

It had just gone 6 am and the depot had only been open for five minutes. The yardies were still walking around with coffee cups in their hands when I arrived. They knew me by sight and that I was trading in second-hand fridges on a regular basis. Which was as much as they needed to know.

The forklift driver had my fridge on the back of the ute in three minutes and knowing that I only had a kilometre to travel, I only threw one rope over the top to hold it in.

I pulled out of the freight yard to turn left onto the main road, but a parked-up road train blocked my view from anything coming from my right. In what could best be described as the dumbest thing I'd ever done, I pulled out in front of a cattle transport road train.

I never saw a thing.

There was a massive explosion of the cabin, noise, glass and steel. The semi roo bar had collected me about where the door hinges were, it spun the ute around and sent me into the storm water drain.

I don't know how long I was unconscious for, a minute, maybe two.

My first recollection was someone calling my name. "Kat, Kat, come-on mate, Kat, Kat?"

It was one of the yardies who had come running out.

It took me a while to gather my senses and comprehend what had happened. A cut over my right eye was pissing blood and I could taste it dripping over my lips. A lot of things hurt and my ability to concentrate was rat shit. I had trouble with the fog and putting two words together.

The yardie was talking flat out, "Kat, the ambulance is coming mate, just relax, don't move. Let me hold this on ya head, you got a bit of a cut. It's all good mate, we'll get you out of here in a minute. Stay still."

I didn't know it at the time, but the driver's door was crushed and couldn't be opened, the passenger door was jammed against the storm water drain. I couldn't have got out if my life had depended on it.

As my mind started to clear, I became fixated on a cardboard wrapped fridge laying in the culvert twenty metres away.

Fuck me dead, the forty-five-thousand-dollar fridge was lying in a ditch. Thirty-two ounces of amphetamine and ten pounds of marijuana inside.

The yardie who was laying on the bonnet, hanging halfway into the cabin through the broken windscreen sensed my aggravation about getting out of the vehicle, but he assumed it was shock and continued with his attempts to calm me down.

He was right about part of it. Yes, I was in shock, but not from the car accident, more about forty-five grand laying in a trench and me going to jail for five years.

I was really struggling to get my act together, my concentration span was about five seconds. I managed to pull a business card from the ash tray and pleaded with him to ring the Dodger. "I'm okay. I need a favour, can you ring my factory, now, immediately, ask for Dodger, please?"

The ambulance and Dodger arrived at the same time. I saw him ignore the self-appointed traffic wardens trying to direct traffic and he pulled up two metres from the wreck. He stuck his head through the windscreen, "Jesus Christ. You okay Kat?"

"The fucking fridge Dodge, get the fucking fridge out of here."

He'd already seen it and was thinking well ahead of me. He pulled rank on all the sightseers hanging around. In his big tough, 'I'm in charge' voice he snapped them to attention. "Stand back and let the Ambo's in. You blokes give me a hand to clean up this shit. Give me a lift to get the fridge on my ute can ya?"

As the ambulance guys were working on my head and pulling glass out of a dozen other places, I caught glimpses of the fridge sitting in the tray of Dodger's ute. The coppers were walking around trying to sort traffic and gather details of what had unfolded.

Dodger put his head back in the window. "I'll get the debris back to the yard and arrange for the ute to be towed, I'll be at the hospital later."

"For Christ's sake get the fuck out of here."

***

Two things saved our collective arses that morning. Firstly, that the Kenworth prime mover was only doing 70KPH and that it ploughed in half-a-metre in front of my head. Secondly, the time and effort that Pablo had put into preparing the fridge with protective foam padding, a roll of glad wrap, three industrial plastic straps holding the doors airtight, a snug fitting heavy-duty cardboard box over the top and another row of horizontal and vertical plastic straps around the outside.

When the fridge was catapulted out of the ute it must have bounced end on end down the road. When Dodger opened it up later it had had more bangs than a girl's school, it was absolutely rooted, but all the seals and wrapping had remained in place.

I was in hospital for three days getting my broken collarbone and dodgy knee sorted, trying to remember where I lived and the gash in my forehead most likely ended any chance of me becoming a male model.

My closest associates told me that I was loopy for ten days from concussion. I didn't look at a beer for a fortnight and couldn't comprehend a tape measure reading at work for the life of me. On a couple of occasions, in my confused state I called the Pom, KGB. That went down like a fucking lead balloon.

I was fined $250 for dangerous driving.

***

By the time my bruises from the car wreck were beginning to fade, I'd been invited out on a luxury boat cruise. Just a quick four-hours depart and return off the Broome wharf. I still wasn't moving right and so I decided a day off from legitimate work and a bit of relaxing were called for.

Beautiful, big dollar boat, a few drinks, good tucker and a look around a piece of engineering that I'd never be able to afford. It was another magnificent day in paradise, clear blue sky, not a cloud for a thousand kilometres. The turquoise water around the top end has the ability to mesmerise the beholder and this day was no different, it was simply stunning.

I spotted a punter sitting right down the back by himself, smoking a joint. Balancing a couple of freshly barbequed chicken wings in one hand and an imported beer in the other, I sat down beside him. He offered me a drag on his chewed-out rollie.

"Nah, I'm good mate."

A bit of idle chat and he gave me the run-down on his life; he was the manager of an accommodation business in town. A bit more chat and he gave me the ins and outs of his customers.

I started to think this bloke might be in the game. When the timing was right I asked him straight up if he got on the gear.

"Not anymore. Why? You got some?"

"Not on me, but I can get my hands on it."

"What quantity can you get hold of?"

"Tell me what you're looking for and I'll ask? I'm told a good quality ounce is going for two grand."

"Price hasn't come down then," he said as a statement, not a question.

"Fucked if I know. That's just the going rate." I was trying to make out I had access to it, not that I was a primary player.

"Okay, I'll have a think about it, I'll let you know."

A few days later I was in town and swung past this character's premises to see if he had any interest. It did cross my mind when I pulled up that this was the same address where the Hashish bloke got busted.

Boat man didn't want to know me.

His demeanour was completely the opposite of what it had been on the boat. He gave me a half-baked lecture about the dangers of using the stuff and how he'd been off it for a while and wasn't interested.

"No worries mate. I was just in the area. Catch you around."

And I left him alone.

What I didn't know but would find out by accident weeks later, was that this prick was very connected to the Broome coppers through a relative and I reckon he set me up.

On the Saturday after having met the bloke in town, I'd driven out of my driveway three times. Being a Saturday, whatever I was doing was clean. I had to swing past work to let someone get their car out and tidy up a few factory related issues. I went to the supermarket and then drove the Pom to work.

The first time I saw the white 4WD a hundred metres away with someone sitting in it didn't register. The second time, I'm thinking, that's strange. The third time I reckon we've been made.

At eleven o'clock, I walked down to the hospital to pick the Pom up after her afternoon shift finished. The 4WD wasn't there.

Next morning, we decided to go into town for breakfast. As we drove out the fucking car was there again with two heads inside. It followed us into town.

We parked up but I didn't see where it went.

An hour later, walking through the mall, I spotted a detective I knew on a first name basis. He called himself 'Drew', short for Andrew. I had lived next door to him when I first arrived in Broome.

Sunday morning, crisp white shirt not tucked in, bulges around the waistline, long pants and a radio in his hand. He looked like a working copper. He walked straight up to me. Using a very formal, 'Hello' and with great emphasis, he tagged my full legal name on the end. He'd never used that on me previously. Not 'Hi' or 'Hey', but 'Hello'.

A pause and then he asked, "What are you up to?" He was staring me straight in the eye and there was tension in his voice.

"Hello, Senior Detective Sergeant Andrew Hahn," I replied, giving him the same formal bullshit back. "I'm having breakfast."

It wasn't meant to be a smart-arse answer but I'm sure it sounded like one.

The penny dropped that the white 4WD following me and the shirt-fronting copper were connected. My brain was racing at a thousand miles an hour. For sure I'd been under surveillance, but for how long? What about Dodger? We hadn't had a smell of green or white on us for over a week and there wasn't any on the road heading towards us either due to a problem in Perth that I hadn't sorted out yet.

If Dodger or I, or both of us for that matter, had been tailed for up to a week then the coppers would have been very frustrated. Neither of us had done anything remotely suspect, nor been seen with anyone else of interest. The watchers would have seen fuck-all, just two blokes going about their normal day-to-day business. Any other week would have been a different story but on this occasion, I was backing circumstances being in our favour. Sometimes you have to ride your luck.

The Detective looked like he wanted to say more but it just wasn't coming out of his mouth. He wasn't smiling.

I had a bit of confidence that I might have been on solid ground. "And what are you doing hanging out in here on a Sunday morning Detective, catching crooks? Can I buy you a coffee?" I asked him.

"I'm working on catching crooks and no I don't want coffee."

We hadn't dropped eye contact. There was a game of mental chess happening.

"Good luck. Have a good day then hey. Catch you around."

With that and without making any effort to introduce him to the Pom, we walked off, leaving him standing in the middle of the mall like a stale bottle of piss.

"What was all that about?" she asked.

"No idea."

"Cut it out Kat, you must know something. He's sure got the shits on you."

"Seriously, I don't know. He's got a serious fucking attitude problem though. Yeah… he's not happy."

Obviously I spoke to Dodger, but I'm not convinced he was on their radar. I'm sure it was only me and it had something to do with that fleabag on the boat. The face to face in the mall may have been a subtle warning, brought about by their frustration at not observing anything, but a warning nonetheless. If I was up to no good, they were on to me.

The Sting

I'd rung Pablo as per usual on the Friday morning before meeting the copper in the mall. His very heavily accented grandmother answered.

"You Kat?" she asked.

"Sì, sono io, Kat."

"Pablo, say, finish. You no telephone."

And she hung up.

Fuck me, what's this about? Pablo was due to put two pounds of "go" and ten pounds of green on a truck on Monday. It should have been here Thursday night. I'd been around to the freight yard at six in the morning and there was nothing there for me and now I couldn't get hold of him.

We had a problem.

Dodger had arranged for Bill and Ben to pick up quantities of both products later that day, but we were completely out of stock. The helicopter pilot was due any day and the Roof Plumber would be back from Derby that night and would be looking to load up his ute by Monday. Our business has come to a grinding halt and I couldn't do a thing about it.

"What happens now?" Dodger asked.

"I have no idea but let's not panic. We might be jumping the gun on this so I suggest we just tell anyone who needs to know that we have a transport problem, might take a few days to sort out. They have to ride it out like we do. We don't want to scare anyone off either, we might be back in business in a week."

The good thing was we hadn't paid for what was supposed to be on the truck that morning. Pablo told me his missus was coming back up here in a week or two and to pay her whatever we owed him then. So at the moment we were square.

"Who owes us dough?"

"Only the Plumber," replied Dodger.

"He's into us for a bit hey?"

"Yeah, I'm looking forward to seeing him tonight. I tried ringing him before, no answer, he must be out of range, might be on the road already.

"He got five pounds of green that came in last week, plus he hasn't paid us for five from the previous delivery and six ounces of white."

"Fuck me drunk, that's nearly forty grand."

"Yeah, I know."

"Okay, tell him the same story. We have a transport delay, but he doesn't get anything else till he squares his debts. It's a good opportunity to rein him in a bit."

"Agreed."

Dodger had been unable to raise the Plumber on his mobile by eight o'clock that night, so he drove around to his house. There was no sign of his ute or trailer, but the Easter Egg was home. The Plumber's wife had a figure that resembled an Easter Egg with legs. Hence the nickname.

She answered the door and was blubbering her guts out with snot and dribble running everywhere.

"He's gone," she cried.

"What? Dead?"

"No, he's fucked off. I was down at my sister's place in Perth and only got back this afternoon. The shit head must have come back yesterday or the day before. He cleaned out all his stuff, took everything out of our joint bank account, not one fucking cent in there and left a shitty note on the table.

"What's it say? Show me," insisted Dodger.

She handed him a piece of paper that looked like it had been torn out of a notebook.

In scruffy handwriting it read, *'Sorry but I need a change of scenery. See you around sometime'.*

***

"I should have let you kill him when you took him off the roof. How much was in their account?" I asked Dodger.

"Fifty grand. She reckons they were saving to buy a house. They were renting that place they were in. I thought they owned it."

"Something doesn't add up there. He must have been hiding a shit load of dough from her. Think about what he reaped via us in the last two years, fucking heaps. So there's whatever he ripped her for, plus cash he had stashed, plus, about forty he owes us. Arsehole could be anywhere by now. What about the builder he was working for in Derby?"

"I rang him. He said the prick dropped in on him for a cash advance on a job, legged it and has been uncontactable. Took four grand from him."

"And his mate, Sniper's Nightmare?"

"Sniper's hasn't been sighted since he got arrested in town with that Hashish bloke."

"Any chance the Easter Egg is in on it?"

"Nup, no way. She wasn't sticking on an act. Besides, you seen her lately?"

"Fair enough."

We both agreed that if we found him, we'd kill him.

The Fat Lady Sings

The decision to close down the business of selling drugs into the community came at almost the same speed as when we first got into the trade.

The detective had set his sights on me. But I had brushed that off. Then Pablo had stopped communicating and a week later even his grandmother wasn't picking up the phone. Then the Plumber had taken us down for forty large. I was beginning to think we were pushing our luck. When a few days after that, Aaron, the journo told me a story about the same copper quizzing him, that rattled me badly.

I'd been driving past the Continental Hotel when I spotted Aaron standing beside his newspaper supplied dual-cab work ute, nice little perk he had going there. He was surveying a section of re-aligned road opposite the Conti bottle shop that I knew was being talked about as a potential site for a shopping centre refurbishment. I reckoned, like all big plans in Broome, it was never going to happen, but obviously someone on the local rag thought it was worth a look. I gave him a casual wave, but he gave me one of those, 'come here' waves back, so I pulled up around the corner.

"Hey, what's doing?"

"Writing shit about crap."

"Not expecting the Pulitzer this year then?"

"No. Hey, listen," he said, the false humour dispensed with, "we need to chat."

"No problem mate. What's up?" I asked.

"I was parked in the car park out the back of the post office. I'd just retrieved my mail from my box and was flicking through it, separating the bills from the bullshit and the girlfriend letters when there was a tap on the window. One of the Broome detectives that had bludged a free Parmi off me from time to time. Nice enough bloke, I wasn't unhappy to see him."

"Cut to the chase," I said. The hair on the back of my neck was starting to stand up.

"He jumped into the passenger seat and spun me some story about being in the area, thought he'd say 'hello' but he was full of shit. He told me he'd seen me in company with you and Dodger at the Shire business events and other nights. Out at the Roey and other places. Wanted to know who you two were."

"You talking about that Detective Andy or Andrew or whatever he fuckin' calls himself?"

"Yeah him. Drew. Andrew Hahn. Sound enough I thought, for a cop, but he seemed to know a lot of details about me, you and Dodger. It set me a bit on edge."

"He knows exactly who I am. Go on."

"That was about it. He danced around with some minor jabber and pleasantries, got out of the car and walked off. But mate, he was fishing."

"When was this?"

"Sunday. About lunchtime."

"Don't suppose he was driving an unmarked white 4WD."

"Umm… yeah. How'd you know that?"

✳✳✳

So, it's almost over.

I flew down to Perth to see my kids and do some genuine business with a variety of steel suppliers. While there, I needed to find out where we stood with Pablo and what the problem was. I hadn't heard a squeak from him in a month and his wife was a no-show in Broome. The only way I could resolve this was to knock on his front door.

There was a camera facing his driveway and another one at the front door. He opened it before I had time to knock.

"Hey Kat, come in."

As I entered the house, he held a finger to his lips in a 'don't talk' gesture.

We walked through the house and out into the middle of his backyard where two chairs were strategically placed in the middle of the grass.

"Nice to see you mate, sorry I couldn't ring you."

"Me too," I replied.

"We're out of business, Kat. I got jumped on, driving out the front gate of the Gunja farm at Chittering with twenty pounds in the boot. I'm fucked.

"They have me on a heap of charges and most will probably stick. I'm out on bail at the moment, but my fingerprints were over everything on the farm and the name on the farm lease can be connected back to me.

"I don't reckon I'm still under surveillance or my phones are tapped anymore because they've charged me, they have everything they need. But I'm a bit cautious which is why we are sitting out here in the veggie garden.

"They still have my mobile phone, but you'll be pleased to know your name or number was never on the phone they have."

That came as a relief.

"The white was coming from another source. The coppers never got me with any of that, thank Christ, but the games over for a while.

"I'll probably plead guilty to lessen the sentence and get it over with, but I might still be on holiday for a couple of years."

"I'm sorry to hear that," I said. And I was, but in a big way I was also relieved. It truly was over now. Or it should have been. Truth is, I was a fuckwit.

***

A smart man would have wiped his hands and walked away.

But we got greedy.

Before leaving Broome, Bill and Ben shared a name and phone number of some lunatic in Perth that they knew from years ago who was in the game and might be able to help with keeping the powder business going.

They rang 'Gunna' to tell him I might make contact and gave him the heads up that I was okay to deal with. The only niggle I had was how good Gunna would really be? If he was so crash hot, why hadn't Bill & Ben had anything to do with him for years?

But I tried my luck and rang the number.

A woman answered and she explained that Gunna was busy, how could she help?

"I have this number from acquaintances in Broome, they said I could drop around and catch up with Gunna."

"Yes," she replied. "I know the story. When do you want to come around?"

"Today if you want to give me an address."

She gave me a northern-suburb industrial area address. Turned out to be a small factory unit facing the street in a shitty area. On one side of the unit was a vacant block of land with a caravan parked up in the middle and a chained up German shepherd going off his head at my arrival. There were three or four cars parked up along the street and apart from the dog it was quiet. Not another person in sight.

I knocked on a hard-core, steel fabricated, front door and Vicki let me in. Same bird I'd spoken to on the phone, good-looking, in her late twenties.

The inside of the factory unit had been roughly converted into accommodation and the first room we walked into was the lounge. And it was a shit hole.

There were no windows and only a couple of 25-watt globes put any light into the room. If the owner was trying to create a 'drug den' environment then he'd succeeded magnificently.

I could hardly see or breathe through the blue marijuana smoke haze. Four scruffy blokes were laying around on fucked up couches that your dog wouldn't have slept on. A table in the middle was a foot high with empty beer, mixed drink cans and bottles. Overflowing ashtrays were everywhere. The carpet on the floor squeaked with stale grog or urine or Christ knows what.

I was on the back foot immediately. This was not my idea of how or where I wanted to do business. My appearance, dressed reasonably well with a collared shirt was at opposite ends of the scale to these wacko's. Filthy black jeans and sleeveless T-shirts, tatts and beards everywhere. One of them struggled to get up out of his lounge chair, a fraction taller than me he held his hand out, "I'm Gunna. We're just having a meeting, you want a beer? Joint?"

"No. I came to talk to you. If you're busy, I'll leave."

I may have put too much emphasis on the 'No' that indicated I wasn't over pleased about being in their company. Two of the other clowns stood up and took a step forward.

I was thinking I was in deep shit and sensed they were going to roll me. I deliberately only had fifteen hundred on me, so they weren't going to get a big pay day but I was sure that a flogging was imminent.

My intention was to sound this yo-yo out, buy a small quantity off him, say an ounce to start with, see how he operated and the quality of the product. That's why I wasn't carrying a suitcase full of cash.

"You look like a cop," said one of them while trying to stare me down.

My eyes were darting around the room looking for something to use as a weapon but a 345ml beer bottle wasn't going to go far.

"Pull your fucking head in mate. You want to talk Gunna, or we give it a miss?" I asked.

Gunna started waving his hands around the place. "Okay, okay, everyone settle down."

He pointed to the two that were standing, "I'll catch you blokes later. Bruno you hang around, we might have to sort some things out."

Gunna must have carried a bit of influence as they grabbed their phones and half-empty cans and walked out without offering up any comment. Both gave me a final once over as they went past.

The tension eased a touch, the odds were still not good, but better than having four of them in the room.

After Vicki let the two goons out the front door, Gunna said, "We need to get to know each other. I don't do business till I know who I'm dealing with. Sit down and we'll have a beer."

"Bang your beer in your arse Gunna, I'm used to dealing with professionals, not fucking amateurs. You know who I am because your mates in Broome introduced us. If that doesn't wash with you, no worries, I'll leave. I don't have the time or patience to be fucked around with. We understand each other?"

He looked over to Bruno, "Stay here for a minute." Then to me, "Come for a walk."

Vicki, the doorman, let us out the front door where I could breathe again.

We walked along to the end of the building beside the vacant block.

"We have a problem." he said.

"Take the 'we' part out. You might have a problem, I don't."

He ignored me.

"See the caravan over there and the small tree behind it?"

"Yep."

"I had half a pound of the best Go I've ever had buried in front of the tree last week."

"And?"

"The fucking owner of the block came back last weekend and parked his caravan over the top of it. I reckon the shepherd has got into it, he's been off his head and frothing at the mouth all week."

"I noticed. Mate, I don't need this in my life, I'm out of here."

"Hang on, I've got another bloke up my sleeve, he's just up the road. He's got ounces for twelve hundred, plus a hunge if I go get it," he offered.

So, against my better judgement, we walked back inside.

"I need the money up front," he said.

I pulled the wad of notes out of my pocket and peeled off twelve one-hundred-dollar notes. There was no favours on the price but this was the starting point and I was aware that was about the going rate in Perth for an ounce at the time. "You get the other hundred when I get the ounce." I told him.

He waved up Bruno, "Were going for a drive." Pointing to me he said, "Stay here, Vicki will look after you."

That's the best offer I've had all day.

"How long you going to be?"

"Twenty minutes."

I accepted Vicki's offer of a beer and searched for a clean area of the couch to sit on.

Vicki turned out to be half intelligent as well as good-looking and chatted away like we'd known each other forever, I quite liked her style. A bit unfortunate that she was tied up with these dropkicks though.

Fifteen minutes went by, Vicki had a glint in her eye and I started to think that it was bad luck her boyfriend was due back soon.

Thirty minutes passed and although I was happy hanging with Vicki, I was becoming agitated that Gunna was missing in action, so I pulled my phone out and rang his number. Vicki's phone on the table rang.

"Is that your number?"

"Yes, Gunna doesn't give his number out for obvious reasons. Anyone needs him goes through me."

"Ring him please."

She did and he replied, "Ten minutes."

An hour ticked over. Vicki and I had been working on sealing our own deal when shit head and Bruno came back, banging loudly on the front door. They walked in carrying cigarettes and two six packs of grog.

"Where the fuck you been?"

"We got tied up. I can't help you Kat. I couldn't find my man," he said and started pulling my cash out of his pocket. He handed me some notes and loose change.

"What's this?" I asked. Holding the coins up.

"I went past the bottle shop and didn't have any cash, had to tap into your dough. Sorry about that."

"So, I've babysat your girlfriend for an hour, no white and I'm paying for your piss?"

"Sorry mate, we tried. I'll give you a ring when the German shepherd dies, okay?"

"Yeah, no worries."

Vicki showed me out.

What a bunch of yahoo's. Clowns of the highest order, feral people.

I'd lowered myself to a gutter level of society that I'd never seen before and I was drinking beer with them. I was embarrassed that I'd sunk so low to search out a bloody dollar.

I'd stooped lower than shark shit, the gutter of the drug world.

I made a promise to myself right there and then that I'd never do that again.

I drove to the end of Gunna's street and pulled over. I deleted Vicki's phone number and rang Dodger.

"Boz Scaggs mate. I'll be back up on Friday, see you then."

Another singer Dodger and I liked was the American Boz Scaggs and the reference was to one of his songs.

'It's Over'.

The Evener

We became respectable. Only doing building. Only doing the dodgy banking like Tommy had shown us. Only dodging tax and maintenance payments. Respectable.

It was all good. Aaron kept us updated on what the cops were doing, we kept him in drinks at the Shire business functions and life continued. I wanted to draw a great big line under it all, but Dodger wasn't the sort of bloke that let a grudge go easily.

His prior history showed that he would take it to heart and see the issue through to his dying days if need be.

When we realised the Roof Plumber had ripped us for forty large and about a dozen other individuals and businesses as well, he swore that he would find him one day and, 'Sort the fucker out'.

The expression was a bit open ended, but I had no doubt if he ever got his hands around the Plumber's neck that it would end in tears. I wasn't all that happy about being taken for a ride either, but I had a slightly more reserved approach in that it was forty grand all up, a loss of twenty each. If you took that as a percentage of what we had pocketed, in cash, each, it would have been less than two percent. Just get over it, wasn't worth losing sleep over, move on.

On the other hand, I understood Dodger's annoyance at the Plumber setting us up over a period of time with full intention that he was going to do a runner when circumstances were right. Plus, the lies and deceit that he'd built into the sting.

Dodger knew he'd been fucked over royally and it ground away at him badly.

We told everyone we knew, far and wide, that our legitimate business had been damaged by the Plumber because we had paid him upfront on a couple of jobs to help him out. It was a bullshit story but aligned with a couple of other businesses we knew he'd rolled.

It made us look a bit naive from a business sense, but that was a better alternative than telling the world it was a drug debt.

We believed the Plumber had moved well away from the north-west, maybe into Darwin or even Queensland. As big as the top end is, its low population with its sprinkling of towns across the top make it a little hard for someone to stay under the radar. Especially in the building trade where everyone knew everyone or had heard about so-and-so. He had to have gone a long way south or more likely, down to the south-eastern states with their big cities and big populations. You could get lost down there.

He disappeared off the face of the earth, no one saw or heard of him for years.

***

We were making okay money, but then we took a bit of a hit. Big Boy Fat Frank had been feeding us his usual insurance jobs all the time since we'd met him. Even when we hadn't been able to get him weed, we'd kept him in beers enough that he still came through for us, but one month I heard nothing from him. The same the next.

I had his business card on my desk and picked it up, flicking it over in my fingers. It really wasn't like him to be quiet. I put the card down and lifted the phone. His mobile number was either turned off or out of range. I tried his landline and a woman answered.

"Sorry, Frank is not with us anymore. I'm afraid he passed away. A heart attack about a month ago."

It was May 1997 and I thought I was getting a bit tired of Broome.

In addition to Frank's demise, the building trade had had a couple of other rises and falls, mainly due to the hold-up on the government releasing land for expansion.

We had ridden the waves well, adjusted our commitments and employee levels to suit the mood of the town when we needed too.

We never struggled with having something to do, but the pressure wasn't always at full speed as it had been in the previous years. Dodger and I had remained motivated but there was definitely a slowing down in the level of our enthusiasm.

Money wasn't a big problem, we had both managed to build decent new homes for ourselves and as sure as shit, we weren't broke.

The business had always returned a profit thanks to the guidance of Tommy and we had continued to rub shoulders with the Broome elite when we felt like it.

As seemed to be the way of my life, several life-changing events jumped up in a short period of time to change my direction. A few days before learning about Frank and completely out of the blue, Tommy had introduced me and Dodger to a cashed-up newcomer to town who wanted to know if we were interested in selling the business. I hadn't given the idea any thought until that point but after the news of Frank and after a few beers later that day, I was thinking it wasn't such a bad idea.

Also, the Pom was driving me nuts.

She was typical of most pale, white-skinned humans who were raised in cold climates and arrived in a tropical heat environment thinking how wonderful it was till the heat cooked their brains.

While most of her working hours were spent inside the hospital with the air conditioning going full bore, she had become very unpredictable when exposed to the heat.

On more than one occasion I'd come home to find her sitting on a kitchen chair in her bra and undies with her head inside the open fridge door and a couple of empty beer cans rattling around the floor.

The condition is known as 'Going Troppo'.

I doubt it's listed in any medical journals, but it is a real mental imbalance caused by constant heat stress. I know of several occasions where blokes drove their cars off the end of the Broome jetty because, 'It seemed like a good idea at the time'.

Another guy who had worked for us drove out of town twenty k's, parked his car on the side of the road and walked off into the scrub with one bottle of beer. Completely delusional and disorientated from dehydration.

It took the SES a day and a half to find him, sitting under a tree talking gibberish. He had no idea who or where he was. It was a week before he could remember his name.

The Pom's climb up the Public Health system ladder in Broome was quite rapid, she was good at what she did. However, she took a couple of hits when her heat-effected brain disconnected itself from her mouth.

On one occasion, during the discharge of the wife of a very high ranking and much respected Broome Shire official she told the woman that she would be best treated with a follow up of, '*Tontine* therapy'.

A couple of days later, the woman engaged her GP on the advice she had received.

The GP, being a newcomer to Australia, did not understand nor had previously heard of this therapy. So, in front of the patient, he rang the hospital for clarification.

He was put through to an English-accented senior nurse who exploded with laughter and explained to the doctor that Tontine™ was the name of a popular brand of pillow in Australia and the therapy required someone to place one such pillow over the patient's head and apply pressure to stop the dopey bitch complaining.

I was at home later that day when she walked in the door, tears of laughter rolling down her face, proud of the fact that, 'I gave it to those fuckers'.

She wasn't quite so chirpy the next day after being reamed out by the Director of the hospital for her lack of professionalism.

I may have mistaken her heritage for the Troppo medical condition one day when we were out in the car together, but I seriously thought she had gone over the edge.

I hadn't been paying any attention to the radio, but she suddenly became very active in poking every button on it. "The 'kick me in the head' song, the 'kick me in the head song'," she screamed.

Trying to turn up the volume she'd accidently turned the radio off. In her frustration she was frantically trying to turn it back on again, bashing every button and knob she could find. She kept screaming, "Fix it, fix it. The 'kick me in the head' song, the 'kick me in the head' song."

"What the fuck are you talking about?" I asked before leaning over, turning the radio back on and adjusting the volume.

A minute later, swaying and rocking in the front seat of the ute, both arms held above her head and eyes closed, she and Rod Stewart, at full volume, were singing in unison to '*Maggie May*'.

The offer to buy us out and the thought of saving the Pom's life came at the same time. Apart from her being loopy half the time, we were getting on very well, so moving her south before my own car went over the jetty was a fair call.

Dodger was in a similar frame of mind. He'd worked his guts out and was getting a bit stale also. He had traded wife number two in and upgraded to a newer model.

He kept calling them wives, but I cannot remember a ceremony ever taking place that confirmed that was the case.

He was having dreams of hooking up a caravan again and doing laps around Australia for a while, which is how he turned up in Broome in the first place.

The new bloke took over, Tommy was paid out a couple of days later which didn't offend him in the slightest, it was time he really did retire to spend some quality time with his own ball and chain.

All our other full-time staff and sub-contractors retained their employment with the new owner while Dodger and I stayed on for 60 days as part of the deal. Halfway through the handover period I got word that old man Otto had died.

As a strange thank you for having looked out for him and looked after it, he had bequeathed me his old block on Clementson. I decided the land wouldn't affect my decision to leave. Maybe it would come in handy in the future.

✳✳✳

When we had finished work on our last day, we sat and had one last beer around the smoko table, shook a few hands and reminisced a few stories that could be told in open company. I took a walk over to the wire-mesh front fence and to one side a slightly raised pindan mound. I snapped a flowering twig off the tree, laid it on the raised earth, patted the ground and said goodbye to the best animal I'd ever owned.

Dodger and I were both a bit melancholy as we drove out the front gate one last time. We decided to pick up the girls and head out to Cable Beach to catch the sunset and unwind. We deserved a cold beer on a warm night and there was no better place to enjoy it than laying witness to one of the most spectacular sunsets known to mankind.

The lovelies took a stroll along the beach while Dodger and I found an empty wooden bench above the sand dunes, in front of the surf club, overlooking the beach.

A group of young children played in front of us, at the water's edge of an Indian Ocean as warm as a bath. Their good-looking, bikini clad mums were keeping an eye on the toddlers. It crossed my mind that the mums could've kept their eyes on me anytime they liked.

The world was in perfect sync.

The tourists who had ridden the camel train 500-metres along the beach and back, had dismounted with 10 minutes to spare before the blazing sun would kiss the horizon. The orange glow was deepening and spreading across the calm water. Even the youngsters seemed to sense nature's calming spirit, sitting on the wet sand and allowing the gentle ripples of the waves to cover their legs.

The faintest of breezes, barely discernible, thankfully carried the heavy odour of the camels out to sea and left me surrounded with the smell of beer and bougainvillea. I could have bottled that scent and made a fortune on the worksites of Broome. I'd have called it Eau de Pindan.

The only noise came from the old pearl lugger with a birthday party on board. It sailed past and with military precision, or dumb luck, fell into place in a perfect alignment of sunset, pearl lugger, shoreline, children, mums and camels. The whole canvas laid out before Dodger and me in our prime viewing bench seat. My mind snapped the view in one of those moments I knew I'd recall for the rest of my life.

As I sat back, stretching both arms over the back of the seat, Dodger lent forward and opened the small six-pack esky he had packed earlier. Digging through the couple of fistfuls of crushed ice thrown on top, he handed me out a can of Swan Premium, our go-to-beer when the lighter percentage beers didn't cut it.

I ripped the lid off and took a decent swig. Looking once more towards the rapidly sinking sun and feeling the relief of having sold up the business, I said, "This might go down as one of the best nights in my life, mate."

As I should have anticipated, Dodger came out swinging, "I doubt it. And you don't have any fucking mates."

"Fuck you. I've got one mate."

"Yeah right? And?"

"He's a fucking ripper bloke. A class act."

"What's his name? I might know him."

"You know fuck-all."

"Go on, try me."

"Fuck knows what his real name is, can't remember it now. I only ever call him Dodger."

After a long pause, during which he drained his own can, he finally turned to me and said, "You're quite a lame cunt when it comes down to it, hey?"

In all our years together, that's as close as we ever came to telling each other how we felt. But it was enough.

Four months later, the Pom and I were living in Perth, Dodger and wife number three were heading east, across the top with their new caravan in tow.

The Pom was watching an ABC documentary reminiscing on the one year anniversary of Princess Diana's death when my mobile rang. She shooed me out of the room so I wouldn't disturb her viewing pleasure. Just as well really.

"You still looking for the Plumber?"

I recognised the voice as one of the other Broome guys who'd been done out of money back in the day.

"Absolutely."

"One of our guys has seen and spoken to him, he's working in Townsville."

"Thanks for the heads up."

I paid for two ATO-provided ABN listings on the Plumber's full name and the business name he'd used when he was in Broome. Both came back positive with an address and phone numbers in Townsville.

I sat on the information for a few days before I rang Dodger who was by this stage camped up in a caravan park in Cairns. I had stalled ringing him with the good news because his previous threat to kill the Plumber had to be taken seriously. I was thinking that time may have mellowed him.

I was wrong.

He told his wife he needed to have a look at a job in Townsville and he'd be away for a couple of days. He left his 4WD with her and hired a car for the three-hundred-and-fifty-kilometre drive down to Townsville.

He found the address he was looking for in a semi-rural place called Kelso, twenty k's south of Townsville.

The first time he drove past the house was six o'clock in the morning. The well-established residence was set back from the road a hundred metres or so on what looked like a five-acre block, the nearest neighbours either side were two hundred metres away.

Two cars were in the driveway, a small sedan and in front of it a 4WD with an enclosed work trailer hooked up to it.

He figured that if the Plumber had work on, being in the tropics, anyone in the building trade would start early. Yet there were no lights on in the house and the small car was blocking the 4WD in anyway. He drove to the roadhouse he'd seen coming in and bought a coffee and a bacon and egg toasted sandwich. The road from the house into or out of town easily visible.

Seven o'clock, nothing.

Seven-thirty, nothing, so he parked a hundred metres back up the road where he could see the driveway.

Seven-forty-five ticked over and a woman walked out. It wasn't the Easter Egg, the Plumber's preferences had definitely improved.

She had a five or six-year-old kid in tow and after putting him and his schoolbag in the passenger seat, they drove off.

Dodger drove up and parked the hire car at the front gate, blocking the entrance. He got out of the car, tucked the wheel brace into his belt behind his back and walked towards the house.

As he drew level with the 4WD, the Plumber opened the front door and had one leg out before he spotted Dodger.

Recognition by both of them was instant.

The Plumber slammed the front door closed and Dodger could hear crashing and banging as he made his way through the house like a steam train.

Dodger sprinted to the side gate in the hope of meeting him in the backyard, but the gate was locked. He straddled the 1.2-meter-high chain link mesh fence, but the leg of his pants snagged on the mesh and he fell arse over, landing on his head.

The opportunity started to fade. He stood up, wiping the gravel and dirt off his face, swearing his head off and watched as the Plumber, in full stride like an Olympic sprinter, bolted down the back of the paddock and into an uncleared scrub acreage.

Dodger walked back and inspected the trailer which had padlocks on the side doors. The 4WD was also locked.

He pulled the wheel brace from his belt and shattered the side window. He searched the ute, cleaning out the glove box first in the hope old habits had lingered and there was cash still stashed in there. Only logbooks and crap.

When the driver's side sun-visor was folded down, half an ounce of marijuana in a sandwich bag fell into his lap. So, some habits had lingered.

The 4WD was put into neutral and rolled back down the slopping driveway till the trailer jack knifed against the corner of it. He scrunched up half a newspaper that had been on the passenger seat, same as he had been taught as a boy scout thirty years earlier, pushed it under the front seat and lit it from one of the half-a-dozen cigarette lighters sitting in the centre consol.

The two front doors were left open to assist with oxygen flow. As an afterthought he unclipped the domestic water hose laying on the front lawn and threw it into the cabin.

When he was confident the flames had taken hold, he dialled the mobile number written on the 4WD door, the same number that was on the ABN report and walked back to his car.

Breathing like he was still running at full gas, the Plumber answered.

"Hi fuck-head, nice to see you again mate, sorry you didn't want to hang around and chat about the forty large you owe me. First problem you have is that with interest, we are now calling it fifty. You owe me fifty!

"The next problem you have is that I know where to find you and I'll be back at different times of the day and night until you pay your debt. And, as a bonus, everyone you took for a ride, including the Easter Egg, will have your fucking address and phone number before the end of the day."

Dodger drove back to the roadhouse and ordered another coffee. Out in the carpark a few patrons were standing around watching the large plume of thick, black smoke rising in the distance.

An old timer walked up and stood beside Dodger. "Wonder what that's about?" he asked.

"House? Accident maybe. Not sure," replied Dodger.

A couple of minutes later he pulled out onto the main road and aimed the hire car north, in the direction of Cairns.

A fire engine from town came screaming past him with sirens blaring, heading in the opposite direction.

Winners and Losers

TC's associates all confirmed that he had been suffering severe depression and anxiety in the weeks prior to his disappearance and that the last time they had seen him, he was clearly in the middle of a drug induced psychotic episode. Everyone that knew him was comfortable with the coroner's assumption that he'd taken his own life.

His body was never recovered.

***

About five years after Daniel, the Dumb of Dumb and Dumber, disappeared, I was sitting in my lounge room watching the six o'clock news on GWN. A story came up about his remains being found in the sand dunes just north of Cable Beach. He'd been identified by an old driving licence found in his pocket.

"Anyone with information should call Crime Stoppers."

A coronial inquest into his death was conducted in the Perth Coroner's Court eighteen months later. I went along.

The coroner ruled that:

'There is insignificant evidence to determine a cause of death. I am also unable to make a determination on the involvement of any other person or persons involved. I therefore record an open finding into the death of Mr Daniel Simmons'.

***

The Roof Plumber's life in Townsville became very difficult in the months following the 'electrical fault' that destroyed his 4WD and tools in a driveway fire. Word had got around that he was a bit shifty and he had developed a reputation for dudding people.

His workload diminished and the number of friends he had managed to hang on to could be counted on half of one hand.

He rang Dodger to broker a deal, telling him he only had ten grand to his name, the car and trailer hadn't been insured, would he call it quits if he handed over ten large?

Dodger reluctantly agreed to a truce, knowing that he was lucky to be getting anything.

The money was handed over at a roadhouse the next day, without injury to either of them.

From the little I was told by some others, he moved out of the rental property in Kelso and relocated south to his in-law's house in Toowoomba.

A month later he bled the family bank account dry and disappeared with his wife's car.

Believed to be living in Launceston.

***

In 2013 a stunningly attractive nineteen-year-old woman knocked on my front door.

What she couldn't have seen while she was in the process of introducing herself was my fingers tighten their grip around the door jamb enough to hold myself upright and fight off the blood rush associated with shock. I was staring into the eyes of a woman I'd loved and hadn't seen for nearly twenty years.

But of course it wasn't. Instead, this was the daughter of KGB.

My daughter.

She explained that she wanted to meet her biological father and staring hard into my eyes asked, "Are you Kat?"

The shit had hit the fan a month earlier at a round table family and doctor conference following KGB's middle child's diagnosis of Leukaemia. The best possible chance for his survival would come from a stem-cell transplant and the best chance for a match would come, preferably, from a sibling donor.

Unfortunately, KGB's youngest daughter was not a suitable match owing to the parentage differential between her and her two siblings.

The doctor fucked up big time, believing that he was dealing with a conjoined family of multiple marriages and hadn't realised that only one person sitting at the table was aware of the true facts.

The revelation had both KGB's husband and the daughter asking, "What the fuck are you talking about?"

A very long and difficult afternoon followed for all concerned.

When the daughter decided that she would like to meet her biological father it only took her five minutes to find me as my address was listed in the White Pages.

She told me later that as she pulled into the driveway, unannounced, she was pleased to note the quality of the house and the two upmarket vehicles parked there.

She joked that, "Well at least the old man wasn't a no-hoper."

The tears that flowed that day were filled with mixed emotions. Happiness that she had come looking and sadness that we had lost twenty years of love and affection that we would never be able to pull back.

Before our second meeting, held in an expensive restaurant in South Perth, I pulled five grand out of my floor safe and went for a drive to see the shifty jeweller I knew. He assembled a magnificent 18K yellow gold necklace with a triangle of three, 12mm, perfectly round, Broome pearls hanging in a pendant. Between each pearl, separated by a 20mm length of gold chain, was a 0.04ct Kimberley diamond. It almost brought a tear to my eye when I saw the finished product. While I was in the mood, I decided to complement it with a matching bracelet and had the words, *'Avec amour, Le Chat'* engraved onto the back.

The five grand didn't quite cover the cost so I pulled a credit card out to drop the balance on.

I brokered a family reunion with my other two adult kids to meet their long-lost stepsister and was thrilled that they got on like a house on fire. Looking across the table, it warmed my heart no end knowing that I'd fathered three good-looking, well-adjusted humans. Without any airs and graces, I let them all know that when the time came, their inheritance would now be a three-way split.

***

The Dodger died alongside his third wife in 2014 when his Land Cruiser and caravan met a road train at a combined speed of two hundred KPH on the Bruce Highway, just south of Tully in Queensland. If the sudden stop didn't kill them, the ensuing fire did.

The severely injured semi driver would tell a coronial inquest that there was a puff of smoke from Dodger's vehicle a fraction of a second before it swung into his path, indicating a tire had blown out. He would tell the court that he was haunted by the vision of the female passenger's face as it disappeared under the front of the prime mover.

Epilogue

Perth 2022

Kat was paroled early from Wooroloo Prison in 2017 due to the aggressive stomach cancer he had been diagnosed with while in custody for his drink-driving indiscretions.

The day I visited Kat, he'd urged me to write his memoirs about his life in Broome, but with a caveat. I could write it, but I wasn't allowed to publish it before he died. Otherwise he thought he'd likely be back inside Wooroloo, or worse.

He didn't give me a precise date, but his guess of six month's life expectancy hadn't been too far off. He died five months after being released.

During those months he and I met once a week for the first four months and recorded an hour's interview on each occasion. The information supplemented the journal and added in later information he had never written down.

The last four weeks he couldn't speak, nor see, but I sat with him. He knew I was there. I think.

At the funeral service, his three children sat together in the front row holding hands. In the row behind them sat a stunningly attractive fifty-six-year-old woman. I recognised her from those Broome days. Most didn't.

Six months later, the transcripts of the interviews and that journal he had sent me to Broome to retrieve had been shaped into the story you've just read.

I think I've cleared up most of what he wanted to say, but there are a few final threads.

Kat's last will and testament added a further rider to his story. He gave me the full rights to it, but I couldn't publish it for a further five years after his death. His reasoning was that if Tommy was still around, by then he'd be too old for the authorities to bother with.

His will also left a block of land on Clementson Street, Broome, to his three kids. He'd owned it for more than two decades. On it sat a 40m square, heavily rusted, corrugated iron shed blotched with the signature red of pindan dust. Inside it was an accommodation donga, the chassis of which had been cut raggedly by a 3mm steel cutting blade. His children sold the block to the highest bidder.

On the last page of Kat's journal, hidden by him before he left Broome all those years ago, was a single line.

Dedicated to my brother, Dodger and to the love of my life.

There was no name after the last full stop.

As for the black bag I also recovered from the hiding place. It was empty. Honest.

***

KGB declined to be interviewed for this book. When I did catch up with her I found she was divorced and living in a quiet suburb in the south-west of WA. I also noticed on the inside of her right wrist the tattoo of a cat.

***

Senior Detective Sergeant Andrew Hahn also declined to be interviewed for this book. However, a few weeks after I had approached him for comment (he's retired and living in a swanky Perth suburb), I received the following in an unmarked, un-stamped envelope placed in the post box of my house:

Your Ref:
Our Ref:
Inquiries:

WESTERN AUSTRALIA 6814
TELEPHONE
FACSIMILE

Case Br/WAP/Sur/1698/97

Surveillance Report on Subject:

(1) Subject and associate, designated *Delta* – (see report Br/WAP/Sur/1695/97) were observed in meeting with known Broome drug distributors in commercial premises located at no. China Town, Broome at 14:40 on

(2) Despite multiple covert entries into the subject's domestic and commercial premises before and after this latest meeting, no evidence of drug stocks, supply or distribution methods, nor excess cash have been found.

(3) Photo-surveillance assets will remain in place until the end of the month, however, without any additional evidence, it is recommended that Operation Pindan is terminated at that point. A full recommendation will be forwarded to the Dept. of Public Prosecutions and a formal termination order will be issued at that date.

Andrew Hahn
Senior Detective
Broome Criminal Investigation Department
Western Australian Police

I have redacted the names and dates but it was a report on Kat and Dodger (designated Delta by the police). The address of the meeting was Bill and Ben's. Also inside the envelope were a set of old police surveillance photos. Paper-clipped onto the photos and the report was a handwritten note.

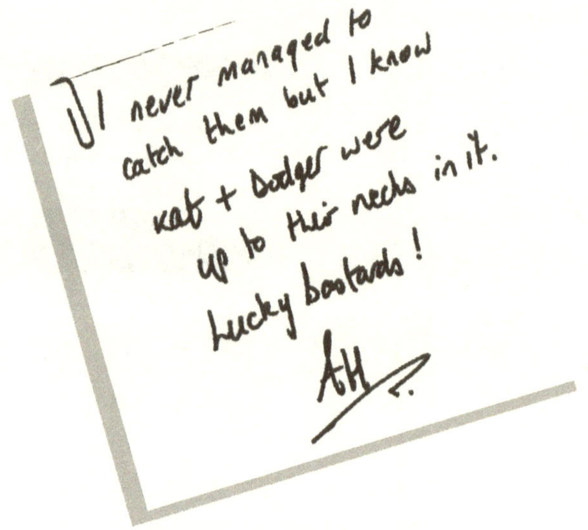

Extract from Kat's Diary

22nd August 1990

I'm starting to write this because I've just moved my life from Perth, the city I was born and raised in, to Broome, a town I know fuck-all about.

I might be here for a week, I might be here for the rest of my life. All I know at the minute is I'm here now.

Probably worse places to be. Looks like the Americans are going to war over some place called Kuwait and some nutter called Saddam. Bob Hawke, our beer-loving Prime Minister, wants to join in, so I figure moving up here to the top corner of Western Australia into a tropical climate isn't such a bad option. Maybe I can put some direction back into my life, emotionally and financially. Maybe start out on my own.

I've always liked the idea of keeping a journal but never have. Don't know if I'll do it for long or if it will become my daily ritual. Suppose I'll find out in time.

Glossary of Terms

The following are particular Australian language slang and sayings that readers might be unfamiliar with:

.05: The Blood Alcohol Concentration measurement which police test for in roadside alcohol breath tests. A subject must be below that level to be legally able to drive.

ABN: Australian Business Number. An ABN is a unique 11 digit number that identifies an Australian business to the government and community.

AFL: Australian Football League – Aussie Rules, Australian Rules football.

Amphetamine (AKA Go, Goey, Clout, Whippa, Hit, Up, Amp, Speed, Uppers, White): Contracted from alpha-methylphenethylamine, it is a strong central-nervous system stimulant.

Arvo: Afternoon.

ATO: The Australian Taxation Office.

Bintang™: Local beer produced in Bali, Indonesia.

Blue: (AUS Slang) an argument, a fight.

Casuarina: The main maximum-security prison for male prisoners in WA.

Cask wine: Wine in a box. A non-traditional wine packaged in a soft bladder, with a release valve, housed within a cardboard or fibreboard rectangular box. Terrific for parties and hangovers from hell.

Cleanskin: Multiple:
Person with no criminal convictions or connections to terrorists (domestic or foreign). Also, cleanskin wine, a wine that has no label identifying the winemaker or winery. Also, unbranded cattle.
Also, Sp. Australian, undercover law enforcement agents.

Donga: A temporary, transportable building. Not designed to be a permanent structure. Usually extensively in the Australian Mining industry for accommodation purposes.

Drinking Vouchers: (AUS Slang) Dollar bills, money.

Dudding: (AUS slang) swindling.

DUI – Driving Under the Influence (of drugs or alcohol, or both).

GWN: Golden West Network - A former television network serving all of Western Australia outside metropolitan Perth. With a coverage of almost one third of the continent it was one of the largest geographic television markets in the world.

Flower Pot Men: 1960's and 70's children's television show. Sp. Bill and Ben.

Mung Bean: Unflattering name for a person of unsavoury character.

Pat: (AUS rhyming slang) Pat Malone – Own.

Postie: Sp. Australian. Post / Mail delivery person.

RBT: Random Breath Test.

Roadhouse: Combination Service Station / café / restaurant / and occasionally pub.

Road train: Consisting of at least two, usually more, trailers or semi-trailers hauled by a prime move, a road train, land train or long combination vehicle (LCV) is a trucking vehicle used to move road freight more efficiently than single semi-trailer trucks.

Root: (AUS Slang) To have sex. To fuck. Past tense, Rooted: Tired. Totally fucked.

Rort: (AUS Slang) a scam or fraud.

Rough as guts: Unkempt.

Sanga: (AUS slang) a sandwich.

SES: State Emergency Service. Volunteer division of the Department of Fire and Emergency Services (DFES), Western Australia's leading agency in dealing with natural disasters.

Skylab: The first US Space Station, parts of which, after its orbit decayed, disintegrated in the atmosphere, scattering debris across the Indian Ocean and Western Australia.

TAFE: Technical and Further Education. A government-run system providing education after high school in vocational areas. While university teaches a broad range of theories, TAFE focuses on specific skills for particular workplaces.

Thongs: Australian beach (and everywhere else) footwear, commonly called flip-flops in the rest of the world. Not to be confused with G-strings.

Two-up: A traditional Australian gambling game where a nominated 'spinner' throws two coins or traditionally, pennies, up into the air. Players bet on whether the coins will fall with both heads up, both tails up, or with one head and one tail. Traditionally played on ANZAC Day throughout Australia.

Acknowledgements

Due to the subject matter of this book and the sensitivities of protecting the identities of numerous people, I found it extremely difficult to reach out and seek historical information or detail from those that were involved and who would remember. Not everyone wanted to know me.

Those that did pick up the phone or agreed to meet up often spoke with ease and candour, but they cannot be named. They know who they are and I thank them.

My daughter, Olivia became invested in the manuscript early. She had spent time in Broome and knew the lay of the land, so to speak. She assisted greatly with 'younger eyes' cast over the story, asking and commenting on the difficult questions. Her editing and attention to detail was an enormous help.

When I first spoke to and showed the background draft to my friend and publisher, Ian Hooper, Executive Director of Leschenault Press, his enthusiastic response was, "Let's do it."

He spent more hours than he will ever admit to, looking over my shoulder, guiding me and directing the story with the use of his own extensive, professional expertise. I am incredibly grateful for his friendship and tenacious contribution to my work.

About the Author

Raised in the Melbourne bayside suburb of Mentone, during the 1950's and 60's, Murray Hall was, by his own admission, an average student who muddled through thirteen years of schooling whilst maintaining his primary passion of riding a push bike. At eighteen years of age he packed a bag and his bike and went to Europe where, "all the best bike riders were."

A wonderful career in the sport of Cycling followed. Riding professionally for sixteen years, he competed at the highest levels of the European Circuit, winning a prestigious Championship of Berlin and on two occasions was crowned British National Champion. A multiple Australian Champion, he represented his country on many occasions including in 1974, when he was a double Commonwealth Games' Silver Medallist.

On retiring from competition, he went on to serve as a highly respected and regarded administrator of the sport, including being the State Chairman for Western Australia for more than a decade, a national track selector and track commissioner for Cycling Australia. He still maintains ties to the sport in an advisory capacity.

His later working life was spent in the manufacturing, building construction and mining industries.

While he always had an interest in research and writing, he had never progressed anything to print. Retiring from full-time work in 2017, he took the opportunity to pursue a desire to bring a five-year project to fruition. His first book, *Walk a War in My Shoes* was published in 2018.

Unlikely Barons is his second book.

Murray shares a semi-rural property south-east of Perth, Western Australia with his wife Tracey and an array of furry friends.